to Nic...
with all ...

Helen Dymond's fascination with Handel started in the 1980s when she sang in the Handel Opera Chorus. In 1985 she supplied the research for the Channel 4 film *Honour, Profit and Pleasure* starring Simon Callow; and her "Handel-Lovers' Chorus", a comic version of the Hallelujah Chorus, was published and is still in print. In 2005 scenes from her play *Handel and Susannah* were performed in London, followed by her play *Handel's Feast* in 2009. For forty years she was mainly occupied in teaching English and lecturing in Humanities; her final post was at the City Lit, London, teaching on Handel's *Operas and Oratorios* and *The Psychology of Religion*.

For Barrie, who went with me behind the Iron Curtain to visit Halle, and Philip who played Handel duets with me throughout our marriage.

Helen Dymond

FINDING HANDEL

AUSTIN MACAULEY PUBLISHERS™

LONDON • CAMBRIDGE • NEW YORK • SHARJAH

Copyright © Helen Dymond 2021

The right of Helen Dymond to be identified as author of this work has been asserted by the author in accordance with section 77 and 78 of the Copyright, Designs and Patents Act 1988.

All rights reserved. No part of this publication may be reproduced, stored in a retrieval system, or transmitted in any form or by any means, electronic, mechanical, photocopying, recording, or otherwise, without the prior permission of the publishers.

Any person who commits any unauthorised act in relation to this publication may be liable to criminal prosecution and civil claims for damages.

A CIP catalogue record for this title is available from the British Library.

ISBN 9781398431102 (Paperback)
ISBN 9781398431119 (ePub e-book)

www.austinmacauley.com

First Published 2021
Austin Macauley Publishers Ltd®
1 Canada Square
Canary Wharf
London
E14 5AA

I would like to thank Fiona and Gerald for their encouraging responses to my manuscript, Monica for advising me as to publication, and Mark for his invaluable technical and moral support.

Frontispiece

In August (1750) he left for the Continent. Between the Hague and Haarlem his coach was overturned, and he was badly injured. London was unaware of the accident till the General Advertiser of 23 August announced that he was out of danger.

(Newman Flower, "Handel", Cassell, 1959:316)

May at last my weary age

Find out the peaceful hermitage,

The hairy gown and mossy cell

Where I may sit and rightly spell

Of every star that heaven doth shew

And every herb that sips the dew,

Till old Experience do attain

To something like prophetic strain.

(Air, *L'Allegro ed Il Penseroso*, John Milton, set by Handel in 1740)

Morell had the effrontery to criticise one section of *Judas Maccabeus* and received the following withering reply: 'You teach me musick, sir! Mine musick is good musick! It is your words that is bad. Hear the passage again. Now go and make words to that musick!'

(James Murray, 2007 Introduction to *Judas Maccabeus*, Vanguard Classics CD)

Chapter 1

Broken Journey

'Can you hear me? Good. You were on the road from the Hague to Haarlem. Your coach struck some object and overturned. The driver and another passenger were killed but you were brought here.'

'Ah.'

'You have cuts and bruises and a head injury which should heal, I think, in time.'

'You?'

'They call me Brother Valentius. Val-en-tius. Can you tell me who you are?'

'Oh, la testa, la testa!'

'Don't touch it, sir. Your head is bound to hurt but you'll feel better with this remedy. Here, let me put the cup to your mouth. You must drink it. Yes, I know it tastes bitter, but it will induce sleep and when your mind is quiet your memories will return. Swallow it all, please. And now lie there and rest.'

'Tayadora, la mia cara!'

'Tayadora, your child ,perhaps, or a loved one?'

'Ach, Tayadora, mein armes Kind!'

'Yes, sir, we shall find her, but now I want you to rest.'

'Ja, ja. Je dois me reposer.'

'That's right, lie down, rest your head. All these different tongues you speak, mixed up with my own. You're a gifted linguist, but it would help me if you kept to Dutch. At the height of the delirium, you were shouting in English.'

'I was delirious?'

'Violently so. I have the bruises to prove it.'

'Mi dispiace.'

'It doesn't matter, you couldn't help yourself.'

'When I was delirious, did I…say things?'

'Of course, many things.'

'I was talking to myself; *you had no right to listen!'*

'Please stay calm, sir. You can trust me absolutely.'

'There's only one I trust. Our Blessed Saviour.'

'We can talk of that later.'

'In His mercy He has saved my life! So there is still work for me to do.'

'Ah yes, your work. Perhaps it was your work that required you to speak these languages. Were you, I wonder, some kind of trader?'

'A trader?'

'I mean, you could have been a handler of goods—'

'A handler of goods! Is that what you call me? A handler of goods?'

'Gently, gently, sir, you cannot get out of bed, sir, oh dear, this will set you back, please don't try to get up—'

'A handler, ein Handel! A very mockery of myself? You think I haven't heard all that? Giving here, borrowing there, stealing what belongs to others, nothing worthy of the gift but all is stolen?'

'No, no, I didn't mean that—'

'INGRRATI! BASTARRDI! I shall never go back there, never, NEVER, NEVER, NEVER!'

Valentius, in the moment before the patient heaved himself off the bed, managed to press a cloth soaked in sleeping draught over his mouth. He didn't stop pressing till the big man's eyes were closed, the breathing almost suspended.

The little man wiped his head on his sleeve.

Chapter 2
The Hermit's Dilemma

Brother Valentius stood up and stretched his aching back. He shaded his eyes with his hand and surveyed the ten rows of young vines winking in the sun and decided that his morning's work was done, for the day was beginning to be blue and warm. In the corner of his eye, he caught a movement through the scullery window, a dark and dreadful shape…Agnes, staggering among her pots and pans. She had started early and was already drunk. Valentius wished she did not so disgust him because he wanted to feel compassion for her.

The work itself was simple. He had only to pick up the trailing vine-shoots that lay on the earth and wind them up and over and round and round three rows of twine that were suspended at intervals between wooden posts. This done, he had pulled off the season's growth of bright green leaves to allow the tight green clusters of fruit to hang freely in the sun, and as summer ripened into autumn, he would watch them swell to a blushing sweetness.

It was satisfying to liberate the grapes in this way. A good time, while the sun rose above the trees, to grasp his own trailing thoughts and wind them back around the central question of his life, the question of his belief. He must go in now and write down these thoughts. The grapes, still wet with overnight rain, could be left to prosper as nature intended. He didn't know who would come to harvest them, only that strangers would arrive, offering their labour to the white-haired sage who was reputed to cure all ills.

The one who had already come might prove to be of service. Not in the vineyard, he was much too stout for that and his hands too soft.

Valentius kicked some mud from his clogs and plodded thoughtfully up the path, his dark robe flapping round his ankles. He was already deeply interested in his patient, who had revealed in his mutterings and shrieks of the past few days a good deal about himself.

At the height of the delirium, he shouted in a strangely accented English about this girl, *Tayadora*, who seemed to be the child of his heart. "They" had shunned her, turned their backs on her and in doing so had wounded him so that he no longer knew how to go forward or turn back, but had come to a full stop.

Valentius had a strange flutter of recollection about the man but could not place it. There was something about him, his unusual girth, the fury that welled up in him, the occasional roar of belly-laughter. Or perhaps it was suddenly catching a surprising sweetness in his expression, as if he was listening to a voice he loved. The voice of a woman, perhaps, this Tayadora.

Nothing definite. Yet he had already given many indications that he was a man of consequence who knew the ways of the world and had powerful connections.

The hermit, pausing on his path up to the house, stared for several minutes across the valley, to a certain crossroads in his mind. He was actually considering whether he should try to cure the patient, or simply leave the process to nature. The man was clearly well educated and clever. And this cleverness might prove dangerous: it might be safer not to restore him to health. His head injury was certainly consistent with a loss of memory, but Valentius couldn't decide if this had happened, or if the man was dissembling, hiding from a life which for some reason had become intolerable. He had already challenged the hermit's right to intrude on his private world, and perhaps he had a point.

And if he had the cleverness to hide from the world, if he was allowed to recover his wits, might he uncover not only his own story, but also the story of Jan-Valentius Bergsma?

That was a sobering prospect.

But supposing the man's family were, at that very moment, frantic for news of him?

Supposing a wealthy patron, a crowned head, had sent out search parties? It might be possible – *rewarding*, even – to send word that he was alive.

Valentius entered the little walled garden which, years before, had been Father Anthony's private enclosure. It was still dreaming in the morning sun. Even on a windy day there was no sign of movement here; the broad flower beds on either side were overrun with bindweed and the straggling arms of pink and white dog-roses, over which purple-starred campion had long ago woven a celestial gauze. These were the very weeds which the Brothers, in their divine certainties, had instructed him to root out, and which by now had utterly prevailed.

He leaned his grizzled cheek against the wall of the house and eased off his clogs. And he wondered, as so often before, *why* should weeds be rooted out? They were living creatures and might have souls. They were no less miraculous than the marigolds he had gathered for food earlier in the morning and which still lay, a little faded now, in a rush basket on the doorstep. It's true, he thought as he picked up the basket, some of these weeds have rather pretty flowers.

He regarded a strand of white blooms that was coiling over the doorstep and thought of giving it to Agnes to tie in her hair. Poor Agnes, so unhappy, so hopeless. Some of these flowers might cheer her up. After a moment the absurdity of this notion caused him to push through the heavy wooden door that led to the scullery.

Chapter 3
Servant Girl

'Pig's bollocks!'

'Mind your tongue, girl.'

'BOLLOCKS, BOLLOCKS! PISSING TESTICLES OF PIGS!'

'Stop this shouting! Do you want to wake the patient?'

'Oh he's all right, he can't hear. As if he'd come anywhere near this hole!'

'All I suggested,' resumed Valentius in a firmer tone but staying in the safety of the doorway, 'was that when you have roasted the meat you make some savoury broth. The poor man is in a desperately weak condition.'

Agnes threw the bloody knife she had been wielding down onto the flagstones where it spattered blood almost onto Valentius' feet and watched to see if he would flinch. Through long practice, he did not. She blew a strand of hair off her face and stared malevolently at her master. Her dark head with its coronet of sweat drops and its misshapen right ear was huge in the frame of the scullery window.

Valentius, relieved that the expected confrontation had gone reasonably well, turned to go. She sprang forward and slammed the door viciously against the back of his heel, then grinned as she heard his high-pitched yelp, followed by an uneven clapping of sandals as the old man limped away from her domain.

Then she moved through blackened smoke to the table and the pile of earthy vegetables she had been peeling. It was while she was chopping onions that she had given her finger quite a deep cut which still throbbed blood, so she wiped it on her leg and tossed the blood-stained pieces into the soup. By the time she had hacked potatoes and turnips into lumps, dropped them with a greasy splash into the cauldron, and bent down to blow on the red sticks which sent hot ashes scattering into her eyes, sweat was pouring down her homespun shift and it stuck to her body like sloughed-off skin.

'BOLLOCKS!'

She tore off her leather apron and the sopping wet shift together and threw them down on the floor. At once the fire shot a rich scorch-mark bubbling up on her shin which she greeted with a volley of curses. But even before she had finished cursing, her face twisted itself into its grin: it bent down between her freely swinging breasts to witness the birth of a new blister on her scabby body. She watched it as it swelled up and subsided, finding a place among its sister-sores.

Agnes habitually squeezed pus out of her sores like honey, and picked her scabs again and again, for every agony she suffered was a denial of that Great Lie the Brothers called *Our Loving Father*.

Then she gripped both hands round the rusty handle of the spit on which two blood-stained hares were roasting, and grunting loudly, she managed a stiff revolution of ear-splitting creaks. Lucky the villagers were stupid fucking sheep! Believing Valentius to be their holy man, they went on leaving gifts at his door just as they had in the days of the monks: and so she had found a precious bag of salt, a honeycomb, and these two headless hares on the step.

The hares settled down to an upside-down position with their necks spitting against the flame. Agnes stood up dizzily and groped her way to her bed, a collapsed leather armchair which had taken root in the large green hole in the wall that was her window. Half-buried in creepers, it kept watch over the woodland below like a heavily fringed eye. She tied her grey-streaked tangle of hair into a knot, stretched her scabby legs out luxuriously and reached for her treasures, a cobwebby flagon and a chewed clay pipe which sat together on the warm window ledge.

'He's in a desperately weak condition.' As she emptied the flagon down her throat, she remembered what she had seen. Strictly against orders she had crept into his cell during the night and taken her first look at the bulky shape snoring under the blanket, a grey head with whiskers sprouting over fleshy jowls.

He didn't look or sound weak, he would suit her purposes admirably, and she felt her right ear quiver, massively, in anticipation.

Chapter 4

A Cultured Man

'That painting,' Brother Valentius told his companion a few days later,' has hung on the wall as long as I remember. Our late abbot Father Anthony was very fond of it, though I always find it faintly indecent and felt it might have inflamed the novices.'

'Madonna Lactans di Leonardo,' murmured the other, leaning his bulk awkwardly on the small man's arm as they stopped by the picture, hanging by itself on the bare stone wall. He was now dressed in a huge robe of an indeterminate dark colour and his feet shuffled forward awkwardly in outsize sandals.

'So you know it? A copy of a famous piece, I believe, that was brought here from Italy. You have travelled in Italy, then?'

The big man didn't reply but continued to peer closely at the painting. The Madonna was in almost-profile, gazing down at the curly-headed, alarmingly plump baby who cupped her right breast in his hand, his near eye looking directly at Leonardo da Vinci as if resenting this intrusion on the intimate scene. The Virgin's shining brown hair was braided round her head, just like the Florentine ladies who had glided about the court of Ferdinand de Medici, Prince of Tuscany. Yes, he was sure now, he had admired this picture in a gallery at his patron's palace, the Villa Pratolino.

After a time, he straightened up, took a step back, leaning on the other's arm, and spoke.

> 'The provenance is disputed. Some say the brushwork is too crude for da Vinci though the composition is typical. It could be his pupil, Boltraffio.'

> 'Ah. So perhaps we can deduce that you are an artist, or collector, or a nobleman travelling for pleasure. Is it not so? That is what brought you to Holland and why you were travelling from The Hague to Haarlem when your coach so recklessly overturned.'

> 'Sorry. Don't understand.'

> 'Pardon me, sir, your Dutch seemed so good. Now we had better return to your cell and re-dress the wound. Why do you lean on the wall? Has your vision has been affected?'

They moved slowly forward, the big man stumbling, as he told himself, on legs that had not been used for the week he had lain in bed, with nothing to stay his rumbling stomach but herbal drinks and weak gruel. He had never suffered from unappeased hunger in his life and had not known it could hurt so much; but he had found the gentle hermit to be surprisingly firm on the subject of food.

> 'Where are the monks?'

'All dead or gone away. I live here alone and practice as a healer. That's why you were brought here by those men who so unfortunately lost your baggage and papers at the scene of the accident. Or stole them, most likely. It's just me now, and Agnes.'

'Who?'

'Agnes, my cook. She has washed your garments. But for the present this monkish habit will do.'

'Your cook? *A hermit with a cook?*'

'For myself, I could live on roots and berries, but my patients require the more nourishing food cooked by Agnes. I must prepare you before you meet her.'

'Why?'

'She has a disfigured ear which has affected her reason. She imagines it is more unsightly than it is. You will need protection from her advances.'

'*Advances?*'

'The poor creature. She still dreams of marriage, but she cannot go beyond these doors because the local people fear her.'

'Please, sir, please can she make me something to eat? Just a morsel?'

'Wait a few days, then we shall dine together. And now I'll give you something to help you sleep. Your dreams will bring memories forward. You won't be disturbed. There's nothing alive here but the birds that sing outside your window.'

Chapter 5
Agnes and the Smiling Lady

When she was little, she dreamed of the Lady every night.

Her pale face in profile, her delicate features in the light of the arched window, gazing down serenely on the big, grey, hungry child at her breast, was fused with a dream about her mother who was beautiful in exactly the same way. Agnes felt sure that she too had a red blouse and the same sky-blue gown trimmed with gold, and that when she bounced Agnes up and down on her knee she would pat and kiss the little girl's malformed ear just like the other ear. Her mother loved her, just as the Lady in the picture was proud of her sulky-looking babe. These two mothers were the only women Agnes had ever seen in her life.

When she was born her father's one idea was to throw her in the river. In the first place she was not a boy, in the second he thought she was a devil's spawn who carried some unspeakable ancestral sin in the blood-smeared organ. Anyway, who would ever marry her? But the mother fought to preserve her child's life, realising after the appalling birth that she would never bear again; and so, pleading and crying, she fought a daily battle with her husband to keep the baby, deformed ear and all. He secretly feared the child might have devilish powers to hurt him, and so stayed his hand. But he forced his wife to keep Agnes well hidden from prying eyes, fearing retribution from his neighbours for bringing evil to the village.

So when a roving trader came along, promising to pay good money for an infant of any appearance and said he would take it to a distant country where it could not be traced, the deal was quickly made. It was quite true, as Agnes remembered, that she was dragged screaming from her mother's grasp before being muffled up in rags, half-choking, and carried out in the night. She was taken away in a wagon many days and nights. In later years she was taught to wring the necks of chickens, and pull the stinking insides out of their bodies, and as she grew into a bigger girl, she was made to do bad things. Bad things.

Her clogs clumped on the floor as she passed through the immense sadness of the hall. She stood still at the foot of the stairs as frightened trees crowded up to the window. No longer did she wet herself going up to Father Anthony's study, but it still gave her pause. Valentius would still be there writing till she called him to supper, so she had plenty of time to look at the picture, hanging by itself on a whitewashed wall.

These days she *hated* the Smiling Lady. Hated her clever, gentle smile, *hated* the babe, longed to tear the dug from its greedy mouth and dash its curls against the wall – that would wipe the smile off *her* face! The angel flew down to give her a baby even though she'd given her first child away with its mangy great ear. S*ent her away*. That little girl had grown up now and should have babies of her own, but now she never would.

25

Father Anthony had seen to that. He always used to look at The Smiling Lady before he took Agnes on his knee. It put him in the mood, he said.

Chapter 6

Confessions

Now that I no longer need to hide, I shall find myself.

It's difficult *not* to find yourself when you are lying naked under a blanket smelling strongly of some farm animal. Naked cometh man into the world. So what, by God's grace, am I then? A great belly spilling over the bed, even after a week's starvation!

When did *that* start? I used to cut a figure, slim hipped, broad shouldered with a fine leg that bowed to my advantage. It was sitting all those years, I suppose, at the desk in my composing room overlooking the busy livery stable. London's refined audience never knew that my music, which they were pleased to call "divine", was infused with the rich steam of dung that wafted through my window!

And every evening I wasn't dining out or performing, I would wait for an important sound, the loud clopping of work-horses over the cobbles as they returned home. This marked my passage into nights of sleepless, burning ambition: *to finish, to finish once and for all without correcting,* without getting up yet again to light the candle and bend to my labours. And so it was that once the stable-lads had gone, I yielded to the comforts left by my valet to see me through the night: draughts of burgundy and white Rhenish, platters of crispy pork, crusty loaves and pots of coffee, cheeses, thick slices of red, succulent beef, dripping with savoury juice – *Ahi Cielo*! Can a glutton have no shame, even now?

Apart from my bulk, God has seen fit to reduce me from big to small. From palaces and cathedrals and theatres to a stone cell with one slit of window so high that I cannot even see out. In His mercy He has preserved my life! And till I'm worthy of a merciful Judgement, it must be His will that I waste no more time on earthly pursuits, but turn my gaze upward, to Him, and inward, to the state of my soul. Here, at least, there's no work to distract me.

Perhaps I should have kept *With darkness deep in*…Theodora's expression of feelings at that point, it was heartfelt and moving but I *meant* to do it as I told Morell, to arrive not at the dominant of F sharp minor but the dominant of E minor as required to lead direct to the symphony. I told him, it had to segue into the sinfonia but what did he know? What did he ever know except writing doggerel verse? Anyway, that wasn't the reason. She was pure! Theodora, my sweet, innocent, joyful girl! She would have sacrificed everything, even her maidenhead for the greater prize of heaven. Don't the English care at all?

But who could have predicted there would be earthquake tremors in London? It was enough to send those lily-livered nobles scuttling out of London to their country seats – so what chance of an audience for my beautiful oratorio 'Theodora'? Seeing the thin house, I joked that the Jews wouldn't flock to see it, as they had for 'Judas Maccabeus', because it was a

Christian story, and the ladies wouldn't come because it was a moral one!

I always had a joke for those dark moments.

> 'O no,' the people say, 'We adore 'Messiah', it's a masterpiece, it's the high fashion, but please, Meinherr, for pity's sake no more religion!'

Well, if I want to set another Biblical story I shall and they'll have to put up with it. But I can't delay. I must recover, I must write the music that I know is still in me, Time's running out, something's happening to my eyes. Mama went stone blind; God rest her sweet soul—

NO, NOT THAT NOT THAT! A bent old lady groping round the house with a stick. And I left her there, left Halle, went abroad to seek my fortune. Only looked in to see her on my rare visits home.

I can't think about her now. Weeping only makes my eyes worse.

Chapter 7
The Perils of Fame

The hermit! Every day he prods me to identify myself, my name, my occupation, my nationality—which is British, obviously. For didn't I become a naturalised Briton? Didn't I kneel down and swear my allegiance to King George and his heirs? I am more deliberately *British* than those who happen to be born there!

Actually my future was settled forty years ago when I first stepped off the boat at Tilbury and smelled something in the air that I knew I would want all my life. *FREEDOM.* Escape from the whims of German princes and Italian prelates, where to get on in the world you have to bow the knee and kiss their feet…at the very least, their feet! Apart from a few royal duties I could live independently– which is the only way I *can* live – free to worship in the Lutheran faith, free to compose the music I love, to make and lose money. To make and lose friends.

Yes, my relations with Schmidt are strained but, Lord – whose fault is that? I've done everything for my old friend, brought him and his son to England, given them the important job of copying out my music. Of course it's hard, I write fast, constantly needing new parts for rehearsals, but I work damnably hard so why shouldn't they?

Anyway, how could a hermit, of all men, understand what it is to be *recognised?*

With recognition comes idolatry, which lays me open to the bitter temptations of Pride. Father, You know I love Your Son and have sought to open the people's ears to His incomparable beauty. Yet the devil finds out my secret parts!

Just such a thing happened on the fateful journey which has brought me here. We had only just left The Hague on the Haarlem road and I was slouching in the corner of the post-chaise when this creature locked its jaws on me.

> 'Are you, sir, I mean, honoured sir, do I have the pleasure?'
>
> 'I am, sir. Your servant.'
>
> 'But forgive me, sir! I have only seen your likeness once in Mr Houbraken's famous portrait of you. Perhaps he has not quite caught your delicacy of feature, though it is a very fine picture of course. If I may be permitted an opinion, your profile is a great deal handsomer, more aquiline and distinguished, than might be imagined.'

A whole day of flattery, I won't be able to stand it! The dead flat farmland outside is more interesting than this fellow. He sweeps his absurdly feathered hat off, scattering powder, and bares a disgusting wreckage of fangs.

'Janjoost Willegom, merchant of the Hague. I hope you will do me the honour of being my guest at dinner.'

Dinner? After spewing all the way from Harwich? A filthy crossing, *ripugnante!*

But with admirable self-control I say, 'Pray excuse me sir, I have arrangements to make for a long journey.'

'A long journey? Ah, I understand! You are summoned to play at His Britannic Majesty's summer palace in Hanover, is it not so? Oh, what will my friends say? That I, Janjoost Willegom, a humble merchant, should be travelling in a post-chaise with one who kneels at the feet of KINGS!'

I give him to understand I am unavailable for conversation as I am drawing inspiration from the scenery passing outside the window in an infinite series of jolts. In fact I am studying my reflection in the glass, which I do whenever my rather handsome head is in view and my belly is out of sight. The steady flow of life passes up my long fine nose and streams out of my thin-lipped mouth, dimpled with heavy jowls, the whole patrician visage framed in flowing curls. A pair of bushy eyebrows adds something wonderfully alarming to my cast, and one can only admire my cleft chin squatting on the cushion of its under-chin. A powerful face, you wouldn't pick a quarrel with me!

The little weasel of a Hollander now takes from his bag a brown bottle, pulls the cork, and his black claws offer it across the shifting floor between us. Even at that distance the stench tears at my throat.

> 'No gin, sir. You do not live in London and have to see the common people collapsing in the street with this drink in their hands.'

To hide his perplexity the weasel takes a malodorous gulp from the bottle, wipes his mouth with the back of a hairy hand; you can hear his mind racing over the various pleasantries he might try.

> 'Some years ago, I had the honour of hearing one of your works at Covent Garden. Oh sir, what harmony you have given to the world! Something about Time in the title, I feel sure.'

> 'The Triumph of Time and Truth?'

> 'Yes, yes! Such exciting music, it must have just fallen from your pen!'

> 'An oratorio I composed in my younger days in Rome that I merely adapted to suit the English taste.'

> 'In Rome? Such skill, such economy! A piece you composed in your youth!'

This *merde* is what passes for Polite Conversation. I DON'T need to be told that my music gives great pleasure, nor should I have to explain to this fool that a piece never ends but grows through a thousand creations from the first. Come to think of it, 'Trionfo' deserves another revision, my best musical ideas are in that work.

For that matter, my whole life is in it. The triumph of time…and truth.

So I am thinking and I suddenly realise my fingers are out of control again, playing little nonsense tunes on my lap, quite itching to get at that box of candied plums in my pocket which if I get out I will have to share, though they were a gift to me and me alone from my Lord Shaftesbury's own orchard…

> 'I fancy we are passing the estate of Baron Wassenaer-Oppdam. He has had monuments carved of all the characters of the commedia dell'arte, Harlequin, Scaramouche, Pierrot and so on and placed them around his gardens. It is a great wonder hereabouts. Imagine, sir, coming upon a figure that seems fully human, only to find that it is made of stone!'

No more remarkable, I think, than my own statue in Vauxhall Pleasure Gardens! Don't you know, fool, that I am the *only* composer to be so honoured in his lifetime? There I sit on a great stone plinth, above the heads of the dancers and revellers, playing the lyre in the likeness of the Minstrel Timotheus. But what use is that to me now? How can I loosen my breeches or undo my knee-straps with the pain creeping up from my knees and biting into my arse…with this *accursed weasel* smiling at me?

There is yet one place of safety left to me, and a beautiful place it is. I steeple my hands in the attitude of prayer. The world recedes.

> 'Merciful Lord, have I done all my work? Yes, I'll adapt, I'll revise. But where is the flood that swept

my operas year by year onto England's shore? And where O where is that exulting boy who swore in the teeth of my father and a lifetime of scheming rivals to hear only that voice, wrestling with it day and night and day again until the blessed hour comes when the hand seems to write of itself? There is an answer, and I must find it! Or I shall be entombed in stone, a lifeless statue, never again to open the door of my heart!'

*

The big man opened his eyes again.

He saw that his kind friend the sun had crept into the cell through the barred window, and that its long pink fingers were spread out across the wall.

They were playing over and over an intoxicating arpeggio in E flat, up and down, soft and warm as a zephyr tickling the strings of a harp. He knew that all the love in creation was pulsating in this chord. He wanted never to be anywhere else.

Then he heard his friends the birds sail off together through the blue of a new day.

He followed their ever more distant trail of song. And a smile spread over his face that made it beautiful.

Chapter 8
London Friends

When he was in the mood, which was often, he stank of sweat and other repulsive odours – and he was her husband! How could she have sunk so low?

That grunting hog Alexander Pendarves, rich, powerful, and covered in bristles, had bought her body from Uncle Landsdowne. She was Mary Granville, well-born and pretty, a highly intelligent girl of seventeen, but without a significant dowry she must oblige her family with this red-faced country squire. When Pendarves rolled over onto her she *screamed* – he in his idiotic vanity imagining her pleasure! She a mere child, and to have this old GOAT heaving up her fundament…when she was led to the altar, she wrote to her sister, she would rather have been killed, as Agamemnon sacrificed his daughter Iphigenia so that the gods would release the winds and carry him to Troy!

And what, if anything, of that nightmare can she now decently convey to her visitor, Dr Morell, who is, she suspects, a stranger to the female sex?

Of course, *he* knows her as the brilliant Mary Delany, wife of Dublin cleric Dr Patrick Delany; nothing of the travesty of her first marriage. How ironic that Pendarves failed to change his will in her favour, and when that drooling drunk died from gout, she was twenty-three years old and penniless. So much for her uncle's scheming. She quickly realised that women are far better at arranging their own lives. Her second marriage gives her daily and nightly joy, because Patrick is such a darling, but more importantly, she has triumphed as an independent woman. She is *an artist,* whose exquisite flowers, combining paper and fabrics, are praised as "paper-mosaicks" by no less a scion than Sir Joshua Reynolds. She has earned the respect and friendship of all the great men of her day…of which by far the greatest in her eyes is George Frederick Handel; and it is to him that she owes this visit today from Thomas Morell.

> 'Dr Morell, you were right to give Mr Handel the draft of 'Jephtha' to read on his holiday, he never likes to be idle, and in spite of what happened with 'Theodora', I believe he is ready for a new oratorio.'
>
> 'Mrs Delany, ma'am, I hope so. Our 'Theodora' was not to the public taste, so I am doubly anxious that our 'Jephtha' should succeed.'
>
> 'Jephtha is doubtless a tragic figure. Any father who vows to God to sacrifice a life which then turns out to be his own daughter's, must be tragic, but I see Iphis as the central character. She may *appear* to be the helpless victim of her father's folly, but I'm sure Mr Handel will want you to create her as a beacon of light, shining through the darkness.'

'Ma'am, you honour me with your opinions. And indeed, with this kind invitation to your house. I had not realised that you and Mr Handel are close neighbours in Brook Street, it almost makes me feel he is here with us.'

He's right, the shade of Handel is always here because he's such a frequent visitor, sitting where Morell sits now on a high-backed chair at her little round tea-table. Only a few weeks ago the great man good-humouredly played for all the ladies who sang at her soiree, skilfully covering up their little slips with deft accompaniment, and then sat late into the night in this comfortable parlour quaffing Madeira wine and demolishing biscuits. But the shape that filled the chair *then* was Handelian, positively overflowing it in his enormous silk jacket lavishly trimmed at throat and cuffs with the finest lace, the three buttons he had managed to close straining as he sat, and the whole effect topped by a full-bottomed wig. The figure who now sits smiling opposite her wears a threadbare coat, a shawl over his bony shoulders, and the wide-brimmed black hat of a preacher. He's like a stray cat which has grown too weak to hunt and is waiting patiently for scraps: even now his eyes swivel round to the sideboard on which Lizzie has placed a dish of muffins and some chocolate bonbons.

Of course she has met him before at Handel's house during their earlier collaborations, but because the composer has always been there, filling the room, she has never really looked at the librettist till now. He seems far likelier to bow to Handel's will than Charles Jennens Esquire, when that polished man of letters offered Handel his libretto of 'Messiah'. Watching their partnership, she remembers, was like watching two highly bred but ill-matched horses yoked together, one pulling back to a stately pace, the other sprinting for the finish.

> 'I think,' she says, 'I shall send for the kettle. Mr Smith was to have joined us; he knows I take tea at five. Something has detained him.'

She gives the little handbell before her a decisive jingle, takes a key from the lace bag at her wrist and unlocks a tea caddy painted with a swirling Indian design, issuing a crisp command to the maid even before the girl has fully entered the room.

Morell is thinking that Mrs Delany is the kind of powerful woman he is rarely called upon to encounter and finds rather alarming. A remarkably handsome woman of middle age, he can see that, her still-golden hair pulled back from her face with a jewelled comb that perfectly matches the pendant at her throat, a green velvet gown displaying beneath its bodice more than a hint of her womanly charms. She's known to be happily married and there's no hint of scandal in her relations with Handel – but it wouldn't be difficult to understand any man coming under her sway.

> 'Lizzie has given me this from Mr Smith,' says Mary, peering down at a note, 'sending apologies for his lateness. He's ridden to the post house to wait for the letters from Holland.'

> 'I daresay he's worried about Mr Handel.'

> 'Oh, he always worries about his master! He behaves more like an anxious son than a grown-up assistant. I've told him, you cannot molly-coddle a genius.'

'But I gather Mr Handel insisted on travelling without a servant.'

'He has crossed the sea umpteen times and speaks several languages! Why would he need help? Really, you sound just like Christopher Smith! Now for pity's sake, while the kettle is boiling let's discuss something more important. My flowers, for example.'

'Your flowers, ma'am?'

'My *decoupage*, Dr Morell. You have not said a word about them, though I have displayed them for your benefit.'

She gestures with her fan to a second table, on which some colourful bouquets in crystal vases have been delicately arranged.

'Ma'am, it's impossible to believe that you have cut these blooms out of paper! Why, they are lovelier than the natural article!'

'Oh, never that, only more enduring. I copy the flowers that Dr Delany and I see on our walks round the lake in Ireland, little purple aster amid clumps of golden moss, figwort, eyebright, asphodel, and then we can enjoy them again in the long, wet evenings around our fireside.'

'This one, for example.'

'The Arabian Star of Bethlehem, it is very lovely, isn't it; and this is one of my favourites, Rubus Odoratus, the sweet-flowering raspberry. My aim is to capture these flowers at the peak of their loveliness, rather as Mr Handel does with his virtuoso singers. Ah, here is Lizzie. Come to the table, Dr Morell. We are informal here, please don't wait to be offered.'

And don't choke on it, she thinks, spindle-fingered scholar that you are, with your bag wig moulting like a diseased hen as you chew and *O dear*, what can be said about your cuffs? The mice have been at them! She lays down her fan, re-fills her guest's teacup and watches him immediately drain it while in the same movement reaching for more bread and butter.

'So my dear Mr Handel has commissioned you to write a new oratorio. He will rejoice that you return to a Biblical subject. I have told him that 'Theodora' will be acclaimed one day: his invention of entirely different music for Pagans and for Christians is masterly. The fact is, Theodora's story was insipid. A heroine sacrificing herself on the altar of virtue! What audiences want is the kind of full-blooded character that fires up Mr Handel's muse – Saul, Samson, Alcina, Semele – all of them racked with passions that tear them to pieces!'

'Ma'am, for Mr Handel's sake I have laboured to give Jephtha just such agonies of remorse as you describe.'

'I am glad to hear it. That a father, merely because he took a vow, should have to slay his own child! Infanticide may have been respectable in ancient times but is an affront to the modern world. Can't you see how it would debase womankind to portray Iphis, a girl who is about to be married to the man she loves, as merely her father's chattel?'

'But ma'am, I am proposing that she should be saved from death at the last minute by an angel. Providing she agrees to take holy orders.'

'Oh, that poor girl! So, to preserve Jephtha's honour, she is doomed to live as a nun and deny all her natural desires? You may blush, Dr Morell, but death for Iphis would be a kinder choice.'

'I am merely offering a…a polite entertainment, ma'am…'

'Give him a heroine who feels as women do! Polite entertainment, indeed! His greatest inspiration comes from characters who indulge their desires and then are forced to confront their own weakness. Think of his Cleopatra in 'Giulio Cesare'; she takes no vow of chastity for Caesar, she *lusts* for him, sir…yes, what is it, Lizzie? Mr Smith is here? Show him in.'

Enough, thinks Mary, poor Morell is ready to sink through his chair. Ever since she touched on Women's Desires. Supposing she told him that Patrick gives her complete satisfaction, often several times a night –

'Mrs Delany, ma'am, Dr Morell, your servant – Oh! It's here in the letter just as I feared, he boarded the coach at The Hague but since then nothing, *nothing*!'

Smith perches on the ottoman and is visibly shivering like a beaten dog. John Christopher Smith, son of Handel's oldest friend. If he has in some way failed Handel, how will he explain it to his father?

'Our agent in Haarlem writes that Mr Handel never made his rendezvous there! Reports of an accident on the road, two bodies, neither of them his, no sign of his luggage, he has vanished!'

'Vanished?'

'Body-snatchers? Are you suggesting his body has been removed?'

'Not one sighting of so famous a person! I felt in my heart he would miscarry.'

'He has admirers everywhere. No doubt he is recuperating in some comfortable establishment.'

'He should never have gone off alone like that in his condition!'

'What do you mean, Mr Smith, his condition? If he had a condition, I would certainly know about it!'

Mary fans herself with unusual fervour. Oddly, the news of Handel's disappearance doesn't upset her as much as the idea that he has confided something to Smith but not to her. Handel, she believes, has an irresistible power to triumph; if there was another Great Flood, he would find a way to board the ark.

Smith pulls a handkerchief from his embroidered waistcoat and wipes his eyes. His normally docile face, offset by a neat pigtail, has crumpled into near tears. Why is it that this forty-year-old composer, whom she has seen conducting

his own operas from the harpsichord, remains in relation to
Handel a perpetual schoolboy who can never do enough to
please his master?

> 'Surely you cannot mean that there has been some
> kind of recurrence of Mr Handel's mental
> derangement?'

> 'Not derangement, Dr Morell, NOT derangement! It
> was confusion of mind after the rheumatic fever.
> Anyway, he took the waters at Scarborough, he is
> cured of that.'

Those terrible months in 1737. Not only Handel, but she
herself, only half alive, the big figure sitting humped by the
keyboard, his right hand hanging off his arm like a glove. A
paralytic stroke, they said, due to rheumatic fever or chronic
overwork or the hateful slurs of his enemies –

> 'With respect, ma'am, you must surely have noticed?
> It seems to my father and I that, well, sometimes he
> cannot read the notes on the page.'

> 'Nonsense! He accompanied all the ladies who sang
> at my concert, and each one gave him a *new* piece of
> music to read!'

> 'He doesn't read it, he improvises. Yes, I assure you,
> ma'am. And there's something else. Just before he
> left London a lawyer came to see him, and now we
> discover that he has made a new Will leaving his
> harpsichord and all his music books to my father. It's
> as if…'

> 'Well, what?'

'As if he has finally closed his account with England! As if he never intends to return!'

A grown man in floods of tears. Mary finds it rather moving and wonders why men habitually deny themselves this delicious release. She plies Smith with tea and kerchiefs, Morell with manly consolation.

Of course there will be some simple explanation. A man like Handel does not vanish unless he *wants* to vanish, and what great artist doesn't need sometimes to retire to a solitary world? She should know. Much as she loves Patrick they sometimes have to live apart and although she yearns for him, the yearning greatly stimulates her visionary life.

Or perhaps…a secret assignation?

Dare she imagine that?

Mary remembers saying at the premiere of 'Alcina', when with bated breath she had watched him guiding players and singers through the most beautiful opera she had ever heard, that Handel was a magician, the author of his own enchantments. Supposing…he only pretended to board the coach at The Hague, but has actually gone somewhere quite different, to meet some long-lost love? For there were loves in Handel's life, she has made it her business to find out about them. She must dig deep into her recollections of things she has heard, things he has told her; and this will help to allay the nagging fear, which she cannot admit, as to what has befallen him. Because if there's any truth in it, that Handel is losing his sight – supposing he's fallen and can't move? Supposing he has stumbled into a dyke? *It doesn't bear thinking of! So it cannot be true.*

Yes, she will have to resurrect some ghosts.

But *later*, she tells herself sharply. Right now, she has to organise two helpless men.

> 'Let us scrutinise the reports from foreign correspondents in the London Press, they are sure to indicate Mr Handel's whereabouts. I shall have Lizzie bring the papers here every day and you, gentlemen, will please be on hand to assist. But I will tell you now…'

With the same power with which she has captivated not only Joshua Reynolds but Jonathan Swift, Samuel Richardson, Horace Walpole, and even, long ago, the preacher John Wesley, she fixes her gaze on each of these poor creatures in turn.

> 'We shall only find Mr Handel if he wishes to be found.'

Chapter 9
The Contract

Yes, it was a good contract I made with the English, I think, turning over laboriously on my pallet with the stone of hunger lying full on my stomach (surely it can only be a few hours till the promised dinner). On my side, I got something as necessary to me as air, freedom to create – on theirs, they got my passion for Italian Opera, and my power to pull the great voices to London…squat, dumpy Francesca Cuzzoni, with that nestful of nightingales in her belly that made her a thing of beauty, the pretty-faced Faustina Bordoni, exquisite in her silver-trimmed gown, painting a seamless flow of notes onto the air – and above all, his high and mightiness, Signor Senesino!

I made London the music capital of the world!

The Daily Journal said the Beau Monde simply *had t*o go to the opera whether they understood it or not, because NOT TO BE SEEN at the Haymarket Theatre was *looked upon as a want of Breeding.*

Of course I made money, but it wasn't for that. My pleasure was in fashioning arias perfectly constructed for each of these dazzling stars, to make audiences gasp in wonder and sob in delight. I wanted people to feel in their bones, as aria followed aria, the heights of joy, the depth of sorrow, jealousy, madness, *all* the passions of the human heart.

And such were the eye-watering salaries demanded by these divas that in ten years they'd bankrupted the opera houses!

But I still say it was a good contract.

England gave me a home and career, I gave England grand ceremonial music that had not been heard since the great days of Purcell. My Coronation Anthems were, *still are,* the envy of other nations, *my* tunes were played at Vauxhall Gardens and hummed in the streets. And with my years of training in German polyphony and Italian virtuosity, a European like me could blend these in a unique fashion with the English style of Purcell, whose work I never cease to admire. No wonder at least one native composer hated my guts!

Pig-headed, they called me, *usurper, tyrant.* Though I'll admit now, I was so much in love with Italian Opera, I clung to it after the vogue had waned. But as a businessman running a company, I had to sell tickets.

And so my move into Oratorio during Lent when the operas were closed. Far cheaper to produce because it was unstaged and being sung in English, more understandable to the public. I couldn't go on ignoring the appetite for that. Starting with 'Esther', 'Deborah', 'Athaliah'…it took many experiments.

Look at what happened when I presented 'Saul'. To show Saul's grandeur I hired the biggest kettledrums I could find which had to be brought by boat from the Tower of London, I imported a set of Hebrew bell-chimes to represent David's lyre – all this cost me a fortune and in the end, only four performances. Then I gave London my 'Israel in Egypt' – what a disaster, carping complaints, the choruses too many and too long...despite all my finely wrought depictions of the plagues of the Egyptians, the frogs, the darkness, the massacre of the firstborn – only TWO performances. For years I didn't know if the English wanted Oratorio or not!

But all these experiments finally paid off; right now, London is still abuzz with my New Sacred Oratorio, my 'Messiah'. But that very nearly didn't happen. The Church Fathers denounced it for using Our Lord's story merely for diversion and amusement, for having its premiere in a Dublin playhouse, for being an entertainment unbefitting the gospel. Ach, if they knew how those words hurt me! For seven years the work was just mouldering in my bottom drawer, I only brought it out again for a charity performance last year at the Foundling Hospital – when it triumphed so magnificently, they all begged me to put on a second performance.

And now I've promised it again for next Lent. The triumph of time and truth indeed.

Anyway it's not true I composed 'Messiah' or any sacred work as mere entertainment, much as I love to entertain. Both I and Jennens had the same passionate desire, that with it we would bring the nation back to the True Faith.

I sigh. My adopted countrymen are free, but like sheep, they have gone astray, each to his own way. Hanoverians attacking Jacobites, Rationalists attacking the Church,

Dissenters preaching in the streets and fields – the authority of Holy Scripture gnawed to the bone!

Most odious of all the Deists who rob God of His majesty, saying He created the world at first but now plays no part in its governance. Jennens' own brother joined the Deists and afterwards repented so bitterly of his error that he killed himself. Jennens, I fear, will never get over it.

The people needed a new vision of the miracle of Jesus coming down to earth to save mankind, and I'm proud to think I have given them that. Yes, Father, I'm proud to have lifted the hearts of the people up to You, to have made them weep for Your Son's Passion and rejoice greatly in Your promise of Redemption. Of course, without the excellent libretto I could never have written a masterpiece. A pity that Jennens took offence at the very thing everyone else marvelled at, that I composed the music in only twenty-four days. Jennens insulted me, called me *obstinate and lazy* for re-using other compositions to speed things along.

But I overlooked this so that we could work together on 'Belshazzar'. After all, his writing is vastly superior to Morell's.

The wordbook of 'Jephtha' has been lost somewhere on the Haarlem Road, but I've already read it, and ideas are bubbling up. I must give the people something new, something they still need from me, though I don't yet know what it is.

*

But why, I now ask myself. Why this urge to make one final creative utterance?

Why do I want to give the English something new?

Do they accept me as one of their own?

Yes, you would say, of course! Recently my Royal Fireworks Music triumphed in Green Park with tens of thousands cheering my music. So many tried to come and hear my rehearsal, the coaches were held up for two hours on London Bridge! This was in contrast to the dismal spectacle of the display, with half the fireworks failing to go off! But even so...

Even so, my enemies call me The Saxon, they mock my accent, my figure – and even cast aspersions on my moral life, just because I use Castrati in my Italian operas. *A fie*, they say *on these mutilated milksops that you are pleased to have strutting about the stage, corrupting our tastes, weakening the virility of English blood...*

Dummköpfe! Who cares if an angelic high voice comes from the throat of man or woman? Can't they HEAR?

Faustina's dramatic intensity astonished the heart, Cuzzoni's fluttery trills rang out with the brilliance of diamonds, but Senesino, for all his maddening self-worship, sent his glorious Alto flying across the theatre on the very wings of sweetness, a choirboy powered by a fully grown man. But there were times, yes there were times when he refused to sing what I'd written, and if that gangling cockerel hadn't already been made a capon, I'd have, I'd have...

You see, Lord, I lay before you even my violent temper.

I would never be English, but I did come to understand them. That popular catch 'The Roast Beef of Old England', *in* which I joined lustily when Hogarth, Fielding and I used to go drinking in the Covent Garden taverns,

> *When mighty Roast Beef was the Englishman's food*
>
> *It ennobled our veins and enriched our blood,*
>
> *Our soldiers were brave, and our courtiers were good,*
>
> *O the Roast Beef of old England!*
>
> *When good Queen Elizabeth sat on the throne*
>
> *E'er coffee, or tea, or such slipslops were known,*
>
> *The world was in terror if e'er she did frown,*
>
> *O the Roast Beef of old England!*

And so on, verse after verse. Leveridge wrote it, Fielding put it into his 'Grub Street Opera'. A jolly drinking song, you might say. But it's much more than that, it's the voice of a people that put a tyrant to death on the block, notwithstanding that he was their king. It's that steely pride in the British heart that reveres above all its own sovereignty, that desires not to bend to foreign ways, but to bend foreign ways to its own.

Roast beef.

Happy days, when I and my companions banged our bumpers on the table and bellowed out that chorus in the "Society of Beefsteaks", contests of eating and drinking in which I outdid them all, for no Britisher can compete with a strapping youth from Saxony. A bottle and a plate of oysters with the first verse, another bottle and a dish of fat chitterlings with the second – then all I could swallow of delicious, savoury, tender roast beef, dripping with juice…Ach, this is madness! I groan aloud amid spasms of hunger – *Why do my thoughts keep coming back to BEEF?*

My FAULTS, Lord. Could I have done different?

I will own a bad mistake which five years ago brought me to the verge of ruin.

'Semele' had scarcely paid its way, because my enemies hired gangs of hooligans to tear down my posters, as well as fixing masquerades and balls on the same nights as my opera.

But I chose to forget this. Yes, I chose to. I sank all my fortunes into a big season of twenty-four performances; but on the sixth night, looking out at the almost empty house, I began at last to take in the measure of the disaster.

I remember how violently my heart beat all that night. I'd never been frightened like that. Because for the first time in my life I felt the long shadow of the Debtor's Prison beckoning to me.

The next day I published a letter in the Daily Advertiser apologising humbly to my subscribers for closing the season there and then and offered to give them three fourths of their money back. I acknowledged the inspiration that their goodness, and the noble character of the people and the English tongue itself has been to my English works. The day afterwards they published their own letter whose very words are burned into my brain. They said they were *touched by the great Master's Misfortunes, failing to entertain the Publick, whose Neglect in not attending his admirable Performances can no otherwise be made up with Justice to the Character of the Nation, and the Merit of the Man, than by the Subscribers generously declining to withdraw the Remainder of their Subscriptions.*

The generosity of my supporters.

FREEDOM!

GENEROSITY!

That's why I've chosen to live there, that's what being British, at its best, is all about!

How could I repay them, but by composing more, and greater work?

How could I live anywhere else?

Chapter 10
Deo Gratias

And at last she staggers towards us clutching in her blacksmith arms a vessel that issues glorious savoury steam – I half get to my feet, then sink down, my heart beating wildly – she clomps towards us, bells clanging brightly from the long-handled spoons at her waist, hoists the vessel off her breasts, dumps it down scattering grease and hunks of bread across the table.

> 'In God's name, sir!' I cry to Valentius, 'will you not say The Grace so that we can begin?'

> 'No need,' he murmurs, 'the food will taste the same without it.'

Astonished as I am by this, I don't stop to question but snatch up the ladle and shovel the contents of the cauldron three, four, five times into my bowl, throwing each bowlful down my throat with a gurgling sound and snarling into my bread.

I feel the hermit watching me with a shocked expression and I don't care.

The woman grins toothily before me, wild-looking and dirty but no more so, I suppose, than most cooks, and I can see now that one ear is greatly engorged like a lumpy red potato. But she's not what I'd feared, a grotesque from the Frost Fair I once saw as a boy in Halle with a monstrous ear unfurling over her shoulder like scarlet bagpipes. This woman simply reeks of drink, a purple rottenness of damp cellars, ugh, in which turnips have gone bad!

Yet no royal banquet could be more delicious than this soup for which she has laboured to save my life. She is kind, then. My heart pants with gratitude.

And when there's nothing left to lick and my emptiness is still rumbling, she nods her head and clumps over to a hatchway where she has left, I see to my joy, a dish smoking with joints of charred meat! This she plants defiantly before me, and since etiquette has gone out of the window, I grab a haunch in both hands, and it must look as if I am trying to break it open with my nose.

Valentius has been plying his spoon delicately round his wooden bowl, trying not to look, but suddenly, when the cook steps towards us, he sits up and glares at her; she still says nothing, her bloodshot eyes begging for what I dare not even guess.

And as I continue my wrestling-match with the hare's knee-joint, a disturbing dumb-show takes place. Valentius motions his servant with increasing urgency to retire from the room. She scowls horribly at him but quite soon turns and clumps back to her lair, though she leaves the hatch doors partially open and spreads her rhubarb fingers out across the ledge, as if, with them, she can learn the secrets of our discourse.

'Let me apologise for the uncouthness of Agnes. I have to insist that unless serving meals, she keeps away from the patients. She is dissatisfied with her lot and inclined to invent things.'

'Can she speak?'

'In her own way she speaks of the things that have happened to her. Her father sold her into servitude. They had nothing to sell but Agnes, it's common enough. Her father took gold under a promise to give up his daughter. When the moment came, the mother clung to Agnes, imploring the father with terrible cries to break his agreement. But she had to obey her husband. The child was taken.'

'The mother imploring the father with terrible cries – you speak as if you had been there!'

'I know all that can be known of Agnes' story.'

'Did the father suffer, to make such a sacrifice?'

'Why are you concerned in these events of so long ago?'

'A bad man, do you think? Or merely rash and foolish?'

'Bad in the consequences it had for Agnes. Although no beauty, she might have married and borne children.'

'But can we blame him for making the vow if it was necessary?'

'It's her mother she blames for letting her go. The father's right to sell her, she has never questioned. Can you understand that?'

'Of course. Adam being created before Eve, it follows that the man has authority.'

'Is that so?'

'Certainly. It's a father's duty to make provision and determine his child's future.'

'Even if the child goes his own way?' pursues Valentius, 'and regards it as a higher duty to develop his own gifts?'

'Naturally, yes! What do you know of *gifts*?'

I suddenly feel an old passion rising within me which I thought was dead and buried and my father's voice intoning the words "WILFUL! DISOBEDIENT!" I heave myself to my feet.

'Must you question everything I say?'

The hermit stands also; a diminutive figure but looking me steadily in the eye.

'Yes, that is precisely what I must do.'

'In that case, I thank you for your kindness and shall take my leave. Now, this minute! Where can I hire a horse?'

'Sir, you're not ready to leave,' he says, 'I think you understand that. Besides, not knowing your destination, where would you go? But I think that now your wound is healing, you would benefit from

58

a short walk. I will give you Father Anthony's stick, a good stout oaken one. You could go as far as the old chapel at the end of the cloisters. It's a ruin now, of course, but the organ is still in there, a fine one, I believe it was.'

He sees a flicker of excitement in my face. No doubt he thinks I'm excited by the prospect of a walk after being confined so long indoors.

'But before that, to round off the meal perhaps you will join me in a liqueur which the monks used to make? I still have a few bottles left.'

Chapter 11
Drinks with a Hermit

Agnes is furious when Valentius walks to the hatch and firmly shuts the doors, but with her enlarged ear pressed to the wall she is charting the movements of her master. She hears him unlock and then open with its characteristic creak the little wooden cabinet where he keeps his secret potions – of course, there are no secrets in this house from *her*. She hears the clink of glasses being set on the table, the bubbling as the glasses are filled. Now, she wonders, what's the little wrinkled gnome up to?

'Why do I question everything, you ask? I was a businessman for most of my life. When I came to live here, I didn't join the Order, but I adopted their simple ways and learned their use of herbs. The monastery offered me some clear answers. But the hermitage is, I'm glad to say, a place of questions. Truth is happening all the time, minute by minute, and will never be complete until the world ends.'

'What CAN you mean? Truth is the Gospel of Our Saviour Jesu Christ! This is God's house, the monks, the painting of the Madonna!'

'The painting? I'd have burned long ago, but for Agnes. She needs it.'

'Agnes! What brought her to live here in a community of men?'

'Our sufferings are not your concern. Your own should be. And I am sure they are less of body than of mind. With rest and reflection, they will come forward.'

'Oh, you can predict that, can you? Like so many physicians, you place too much faith in science!'

'Have you known many physicians, then?'

'My father was a surgeon, so skilled that he once removed the blade of a sword from the stomach of a man who had swallowed it. Little by little, over the months he eased it out. And the man lived. But my father placed less faith in his own remarkable skill than in Divine Providence. And he did something a mere *scientist* would never do, he treated his poorest patients free of charge. He lived by Christian love and charity, and I try to follow his example.'

The patient is dimly aware that he is becoming loose tongued, straying into areas of his private life that he had not intended. He is also aware of another side of the story that he is not telling, a painful battle of wills between a musical boy and a father determined his son should have a career in the law.

'Let me top up your glass. So, you reject science as an explanation?'

'Sir Isaac Newton himself said he could not imagine a world as orderly as ours could have occurred by natural cause alone.'

'Really? How interesting. Finish your drink and tell me more.'

Agnes, who has been thrilled with the sound of her own name on the stranger's lips, strains her ears to hear it again. She hears the liquid in the big man's mouth being savoured, and then swallowed...then the flicker of a yawn play about his mouth. Even though most of his words are gibberish, she can clearly hear that his speech is slowing down, becoming less distinct.

'The great Luther held up music as evidence of the Divine Order. He taught us that from the beginning of the world, music has been installed and implanted in all creatures, for nothing in earth or heaven is without harmony – though most people make too much of their own noise to stop and listen to it! Have you never read Kepler, the 'Harmonices Mundi'? He shows that the very orbits of the planets correspond to the intervals of the musical scale. As if this could be by chance! You ask me if I reject science – no! Music is a science precisely because it is created in heaven.'

'You amaze me, sir.'

'This is why one of today's best composers concluded his masterpiece with an Amen Chorus devised as a fugue, one single melodic phrase worked into a huge variety of forms. Do you understand? He was paying his own tribute to the infinite works of God. Yes, I assure you, sir, I happen to know this work very well. You see, the worshippers of Reason talk about the structure of things but know nothing of their purpose. Why else than for union with that Divine mystery we call God, should a composer strive all his life long to create perfection? Because God has gifted him with the supreme pleasure of giving pleasure!'

'Why else should a composer create music? I suppose he might do it merely to earn a living. But for the moment I can't answer that question.'

Agnes hears the big man smile with a trace of pity.

'Perhaps in return for your hospitality, before I leave this place, I will render you the service of answering it for you. And now if you don't mind, sir, I'm rather sleepy, and as it's warmer here than in my cell, perhaps I might have a little rest in this chair.'

Agnes hardly breathes as she waits for her master to quit the room. This might be her best chance...to do what? At least she will look at the man, scan his peaks and contours, fix his image in her mind, let her ear feast on the delicious rumble of his snoring, perhaps even touch him in the way she knows best.

But Valentius doesn't leave.

He, too, seems to be keeping watch, he too seems to be listening. And he feels gratified to know that in spite of himself the man, who is already asleep and dreaming, has finally revealed who he is.

Chapter 12
Melt Your Lips

I am watching myself rather anxiously as a junior violinist in the Hamburg Opera. The evening performance has finished, Keiser has brought the orchestra to its feet for the second time this week, the Goosemarket audience is fanning out noisily to bars and restaurants, my fellow musicians hurry away to the taverns to rent women and drink themselves senseless.

But I, alone of their number, walk the innumerable little bridges over the canals where black water slaps and splashes. I'm a shadow, I'm invisible, so let them laugh, let them wonder.

After an evening of scraping catgut, it's a pleasure to compose in my head or even just think about composition. Contrapuntal music in its pure form is finished! Initially I was disgusted, then intrigued, to find that here everything is mixed together, Venetian libretto and French ballet, German recitative and Italian aria, the classical laced with the raciest folk songs – and the more extravagance in staging the better, these Hamburgers are happy to pay for a show. Keiser, the opera director, has shown me the way with his dazzling colours, trumpets and horns not merely in fanfares but integrated into arias, extraordinary use of woodwind with multiple bassoons and flutes,

and now – Mattheson's opera, 'Cleopatra' – And pretty soon *mine* will be finished...

ALMIRA, QUEEN OF CASTILE

With superb music by

GEORG FRIDERIC HÄNDEL

Almira! Almira! Almira! Almira! Almira!

Don't I realise how open to attack I am, walking alone in the docks like this? I could be set upon and robbed, thrown into the water. I have an almost angelic sweetness about my mouth and soft, soulful eyes. Mattheson thinks nothing of giving me a playful slap. Tomorrow I'll call at his house for dinner, will be goaded by him into an arm-wrestling match or a contest of skills on the keyboard which I will have to let him win.

Johann Mattheson is breaking me in like a colt.

'You must learn to fight your corner, Georg, not sit there like a pudding waiting for money to walk into your pocket. I've done all I could, got you a job at the opera, given you some of my pupils.'

'Yes, I know, and I'm grateful.'

'And Georg, you've got to learn to *flirt* with the young ladies, that's why they have harpsichord lessons, for God's sake.'

I have, or imagine that I have, proposed to one of my girl pupils. But her family opposes their daughter's engagement to me, a struggling young musician.

> 'My dear Georg, the only possible partner for you is a cello. Something you can hold between your knees for an hour and put away in a box at night!'

> 'Please, Johann, what do you think of my improvements to 'Almira'?'

> 'Terrible. Too long, too much harmonic development. This isn't one of your church services, you've got to grab the audience by the balls. Look, this aria doesn't da capo, it decapitates itself. Remember what I told you, THE SIMPLE MELODIC LINE!'

It's that scene, the Masque of the Continents. I shiver, thinking of Mattheson's plans for it. Twelve well-built blackamoors processing across the stage in tiger-skins, their limbs shining with oil as they carry the goddess Africa on their shoulders, trumpets ringing, drums thundering – the spirit of Europa borne aloft to a marching oboe consort – the mysterious spirit of Asia drawn in a chariot to the insistent beat of side-drums, the wailing of fifes, the crashing of cymbals, nothing spared, nothing.

Yes, it's Mattheson, not the modish young ladies whose hands I kiss, who rouses my fire, and moving alone among the warehouses of the port I can't think of him without my cheeks burning in a kind of fury. He asks so much and is never, never satisfied! And just as he helps me, I am helping him too with some tips on contrapuntal writing. We are helping each other, as friends do.

Then an unnatural thought stab at me – *Do we need each other to be complete?*

A four-legged creature?

One night in these solitary wanderings round the town, I stumble upon a shop of eastern curiosities, a place where sailors go to sell souvenirs of their voyages.

In the window there is a wooden carving that fascinates, and revolts, me. A lewd idol such as I've never seen before, with a wicked laughing face, and wild hair, and four sets of limbs flying at impossible angles from its slender, sinuous, boyish, girlish body…

An abomination of the human form created in God's image!

Abomination! Abomination! Abomination! Abomination!

*

From my seat at the harpsichord, I watch 'Cleopatra' reaching its dramatic climax.

Onstage, lit by flickering candles, Johann is singing the role of Anthony which he has written for himself; he grasps the bloody dagger to his chest, reins in his powerful tenor to breathe sobs into the dying aria, crumples down. The audience is hushed – then roars its approval. Our hero jumps to his feet, bows deeply to this side and that, runs into the wings…and here he is now flinging aside the crimson curtain, striding up to the harpsichord to take my place at the continuo as he always does at this point in the opera, but tonight…tonight…

Tonight he tries to push me off the stool…and I do not move! Something has happened! The beginning of myself, I think. I will always remember that day in Hamburg, the fifth of December 1704, because it was so nearly my last day in this world.

> 'Get off! *Vollidiot Wichser*! Think you're somebody, don't you, because you steal my prize pupils – damn you, I said get off that stool! What? Is *il mio carissimo Giorgio* waiting for his Medici prince to rescue him? Don't think we don't all know, the Prince has been sending you nosegays, begging you to go and stay with him in *La Bella Firenze?*'

And now it's after the show and we're two sweating young men snarling, circling, in the stinging night air of the Goose Market and our blades are up, not yet touching. The crowd who have poured out of the opera house are milling around placing bets. Here's a rousing end to the evening, what's the quarrel? Rivals in love, a girl?

Suddenly we're bellowing like young bulls, our swords crashing against each other – Mattheson's eyes are slits of madness! And it flashes through my mind *This isn't a stage fight, this is real…and I'm gonna die!*

CLANG! A massive blow on my chest and his blade snaps clean in two on the brass button of my coat; the spent sword drops to the ground. And together we come out of our dream.

We are panting. We turn away. There's a sigh from the crowd.

I forgave him almost at once. (Later in life I forgave no one). I remember a tearful embrace, loud laughter, a night's drinking together knee-deep in Rhenish, and we were better friends than ever.

For how could my Fernando be sung by anyone but Johann? I'd composed Almira and Fernando's duet especially for him! It was him, only him, I heard singing:

> *Look your glancing eyes on me,*
>
> *Melt your lips, dewy kisses,*
>
> *Talk and joke, laugh and hug,*
>
> *And bring forth perfect bliss.*

When he published his Twelve Harpsichord Suites, he sent them to me; I was living in London by then. I sat down and played them all from beginning to end. I could hear all he'd taken from Froberger, Buxtehude, Boehm, Kuhnau (and they say *I* steal other's work!) But it's the melodies, the pure melody caught from his Hamburg days, and the absurd musical jokes, bizarre key changes, a deliberately wrong accidental at the cadence.

Above all the Gigue from the E minor suite, a wistful little canon dancing its way down the keys…just like Johann dancing down the aisle of the opera house waving his arms in imitation of Keiser. I still play that piece sometimes.

He's written to me; he's a famous authority on music now. He married the daughter of the English Resident but has never visited England, which is strange, since I live there. He wanted to write my biography, was upset when I refused. And he asked me to endorse his theories on the teaching of Greek Modes in composition.

I don't see the point. I find his appeals for my support, depressing.

Chapter 13
Finding My Feet

I had a snooze after dinner, sitting there in my chair, and it must have been quite a long one because when I woke, the sun was setting through the latticed windows. And it's left me a bit light-headed. Normally I'm strong as an ox. Since straining my hand in '37 I've never had much as a day's illness and feel sure the annoying eye trouble will pass after this extended holiday. So I'm quite surprised to find that my head starts to throb, and the ground rises unsteadily under my sandals as I hobble along heavily with the stick. It seems a long way down the hall to the door...but I reach it at last and when I pull it open, I step out into something I've almost forgotten...

The evening air! Warm, and alive! AH! The romance of my younger life comes flooding back to me on wafts of wild thyme and cypress...

I'm standing on the stage of the San Giovanni Grisostomo theatre, my stomach tight, shoulders thrown back, applause welling up night after night as my comic opera 'Agrippina' sweeps Venice into the lagoon – and with the cry *"Viva, il caro* Sassone! *Long Live the Beloved Saxon"* echoing through the crowd, the city yields me all her star-scented darkness!

Huge white moths explode like ordinance in the flambeaux, that dangerously talented youth Domenico Scarlatti holding a posy of gardenias, stares at me from the pit with his eyes on fire; and in their lighted box the Doge and his ladies have graciously lowered their jewelled visors to let me see their smiles.

I sweep my deep obeisance to one side and the other and think: *This is the ecstasy…*

Did I crave that? Perhaps I did, but not for fame, which has always bored me.

The craving was for the secrets of my musical heart to be heard and loved, and I have that still. That's why I go on composing, when the world has changed so much and so have I.

I lower myself onto a bench facing the moonlit chapel. The bench creaks under my weight and causes a flock of roosting pigeons to flap up into the sky, then flutter back down again cooing with indignation. I remember this is the same pleasant sound that woke me up in the morning. How good it is now to be able to sit and watch their important little promenades, their apologetic bowings and murmurings, as one by one they find their places and settle down to roost.

I look up at the bell of the old chapel, silent in its halo of moonbeams. What was it the old man said? There's an organ, ruined now, but a good one in its day. How odd, that I should be directed towards an instrument that is almost part of myself. How much does this hermit really know? And what can I make of his religious life? He utters not a single prayer, never reads a Holy Book – yet he lives in a monastery and sends me to the chapel!

Now I must go inside and kneel humbly, more humbly than I have ever done, before my waiting, gracious Lord. And later still, I will make the acquaintance of the organ. Even in the dark I'll be able to feel with my hands whether the mechanism is still intact. And if God guides me to do so, I will ask Valentius to fetch me a boy.

Chapter 14

A Woman's Vision

'Dear sister, of all my many achievements my proudest boast is to be chief among Handel's women! He would be everything in the world to me, did I not love Patrick so dearly.

'Are you as impatient as I am for his return? To feel deliciously smug, sitting in just the right position at the opera house so that the dear man cannot fail to see us applauding? Oh, how it must encourage him to hear us crying *Bravissimo!* over the shameful hissing of those who try to break him merely because he serves the King, who cheer Bononcini's operas merely to get favours from that fool the Prince of Wales...

'And now, my dear Anne, you see how complete the trust between us is, when I cry from the bottom of my heart DAMN HANOVER, damn the endless squabbles of father and son!'

Mary breaks off as she becomes aware that Smith and Morell are debating whether to attract her attention. Lizzie has shown them over to one side of the table, where they are deep in the pages of the London Gazette, and on the other side she has begun her letter to her sister. After all, with two men to comb the news reports, it behoves her to keep her mind fresh and clear, write letters or attend to her toilette, until her judgment is called for.

'Another one from Holland, Mr Smith? Please read it out.'

'But ma'am, Dr Morell and I doubt this can help us to find Mr Handel.'

'Read it out, if you please. Events have a way of being connected that is not always apparent.'

'Very well, ma'am. *"The States General having taken into consideration the ill consequences that attend marriages of Protestants to Roman Catholics, have lately decreed that, though their High Mightiness's do not expressly forbid those marriages, yet they cramp them with so many clauses that contracting them will become almost impossible".'*

There is a pause while Mary frowns, tapping her fan slowly on her cheek. Smith eases his neck from side to side. Morell wonders if they will have to continue until all the papers have been examined, or, preferably, adjourn for dinner.

'You see, ma'am,' he ventures at last, 'there is no connection here.'

'No,' she concedes, 'one cannot imagine that at his time of life, Mr Handel is scouring the cities of Holland for a bride, even a thorough-going Protestant one. Though I must observe in passing, how very like our Parliament of devious men is this one in Holland, not expressly *forbidding* a relaxation of the marriage laws but *strangling* it with conditions. One woman in government would shake them so that their addled brains fell out of their ears!'

Morell disagrees with a shudder, remembering the vacillations in the reign of Queen Anne: that weak-bodied and weak-minded monarch did not, in his view, prove that women could rule. Mrs Delany has many friends at Court, but they somehow turn a blind eye whenever she flouts convention. He knows the shocking story that she led a delegation of women to besiege the House of Lords, demanding their right to witness the proceedings, and he is now more inclined to believe it. It was said that at her direction the ladies crammed into the visitor's gallery wearing unhooped gowns – just as she later advised Handel, to get a capacity audience for 'Messiah'.

Smith and Morell having disappeared again behind the broadsheets, Mary loses no time in resuming the meditation to her sister on her favourite topic.

'As to other women, his affairs with his singers were always brief – except for Madam Susannah, but that wasn't an affair in the usual sense.'

It was that mention of *marriage*, an unimportant aside, which has stirred this up again. Susannah Cibber is someone she refuses to think about at the moment, it's too complicated, it still rankles.

But…could it be that woman whom many suppose dead and who has not been heard of for years – *Vittoria Tarquini?*

It was said when he arrived in Hanover, she followed him there, and it was all over the court that she was "Handel's lover".

Could she be living in Holland? Has she been yearning for him all this time?

Mary lays down her pen, rather shaken to find that a vision is unfolding with erotic force in her mind: she is aware that she has been missing Patrick's attentions of late. Surely there is nothing wrong in a woman even of her intellectual stature indulging in fantasy…and in her present mood, it would be an elaborate one.

*

Vittoria's pet name at the Medici court was *La Bambagia* which, Mary discovered, meant cotton wool. Judging by her name she was soft, creamy, bosomy, with enfolding arms, a lustrous blonde perruque curling invitingly over her ample décolletage.

Poor Mr Handel, this cotton wool creature must almost have smothered him!

La Bambagia had, for sure, spent the previous hour in delicious anticipation, massaging her shoulders and breasts with oil of jasmine, applying Turkish rouge, belladonna and kohl for the mystery of her eyes. She was smiling as she advanced across the room carrying a sheet of music to give to the red-faced, slightly sweating juvenile seated at the harpsichord. Despite his shyness, or perhaps because of it, the powerful and tender music issuing from his fingers, combined with his manly form, could excite her as no other.

The youth, suddenly remembering his humble status in relation to her elevated one, scrambled to his feet and swept the elaborate bow he had been taught on his arrival in Florence; but the Signora's smile only broadened as she drew his head gently up and raised her jewelled fingers, in their delicate black lace, to his mouth. It amused her to see his eyes flickering wildly at this intimacy. After six months at court, he still did not know how to deal with her; nor, she calculated, would he finally be able to resist.

> '*Caro* Signor Endell,' she purred, 'Forgive me. I am late for my lesson because the Prince commanded my presence while he waited for his boy. Now they have gone walking in the garden and I am free, at last, for you.'

The youth already knew enough Italian and had overheard enough whispering to know what this meant. Prince Ferdinand de Medici kept Vittoria (wife of a gentleman at court) as chief among his mistresses, but he had lately become infatuated with *his boy,* Cecchino, a third-rate castrato from a provincial playhouse, and since it was the hour for taking the boy to his private gardens, Vittoria could slip away like a cat on heat to the music room.

'The Signora has prepared the voice? Some scales and divisions, perhaps?'

He bowed again, but more briefly, took the proffered manuscript of 'Rodrigo', sat down on the stool, and scanned her hastily scrawled revisions to the duet. They both knew that her warm-up routine needed no supervision, as she was a soprano vastly experienced in operatic roles. At the age of nearly forty, this *Brava Cantatrice* had succeeded in capturing the Prince's heart when she sang at the Venice Carnival; she had lost no time in prizing a diamond worth a hundred scudi out of him and was well on the way to wrecking his marriage.

The young composer of 'Rodrigo' busied himself with the score, inwardly flustered. He was aware of the delicacy of the situation and wished that something in his quiet and studious life had prepared him for it. This woman, who was clearly intent on forming a liaison with him, was mistress to his host, whose patronage he sorely needed! He had accepted Medici's invitation to the Villa Pratolino for one reason, he told himself, to advance his career, to learn the Italian style at first hand from the great ones, Alessandro Scarlatti, Cristofori, Perto, Pasquini, Marcello, who were given leave to stroll about the palace like kings.

He had to admit their music was warm with sunlight, that the Italian language rolled on their tongues as soft as peaches. Now he was learning to impregnate their feminine sweetness with his own Saxon power and precision. In his idle hours he too was free to wander in the colonnades and galleries, to admire the Raphaels, the del Sartos, the priceless collection of music in the Prince's library. But already he knew that the Medici splendour wouldn't hold him long, he was laying greater plans. The only annoyance was to find that Scarlatti was no longer there but was living in Urbino from which it was said, he sent begging letters to the Prince for money to feed his wife and numerous children.

Had the man no pride?

So much for the wedded state!

The youth congratulated himself that so far he had avoided domestic commitments. He would have to avoid a fiasco with La Bambagia, as she was instrumental to his ambition. It was her influence with the Prince that had led to this commission, 'Rodrigo', his first opera on Italian soil. He could not avoid this tete a tete but was uncomfortably aware that she identified herself far too much with the heroine, Esilena, in her expressions of passionate despair.

> *'If a meek tear can soften your anger* she sang, *if a heart's repentance is pleasing to you, consider, I pray you, the heart of—*'VITTORIA! Ah Giorgio, it is I, Vittoria, who offers you up my heart!'

> 'Signora, you sing my music delightfully. But let us not confuse art with life. In the opera you are Esilena, the suffering wife of Rodrigo.'

> 'No. No. I am Vittoria who adores you, *bellissimo Giorgio*, hold me against your heart!'

> She endeavoured to enfold him in her soft white arms, to seek his lips with her lips.

> 'Signora, I beg leave, this cannot be!'

> 'Why, when your cheeks are flushed with pleasure? Don't deny yourself, *bell'uomo*, for I give you pleasure, do I not?'

> 'Ravishing creature, your beauty is distracting my senses, but there is so little time to rehearse, I fear we must give desire second place. *All'ora*, it is the

Second Act and Esilena pleads with the gods to spare her beloved husband—'

'Beloved!' cried Vittoria, digging her fingernails into his neck, 'do you even know the meaning of the word? Is that why you have subtitled your opera *To conquer oneself is the greatest victory?* What are you,' she shrieked, 'a MONK?'

'Vincer se stesso la maggior vittoria... Signora, *le maggior vittoria* is none other than yourself, who would inflame the passion of any man. But I must consider the risk of compromising you, Signora, His Highness could walk in at any moment.'

'Don't even think of it. *Ahi, Caro*, you are a child in the ways of love,' she said, smiling again as, with her ear pressed to his broad chest, she felt his breath coming unevenly.

'Is it,' he whispered brokenly, 'a weakness in me?'

'Don't fret, it's often thus with young men. You are innocent,' she said, feeling his hand twisting strongly around hers and squeezing it too tightly, 'there's no shame in giving ourselves to one another.'

'Not here, perhaps, but in my home town, in my faith, to couple with a married woman – oh, Signora!'

For how could he, muses Mary, even supposing that he wanted to, spank her furry bottom and throw her off his lap, when she was *Maitresse-en-Titre to* his patron?

Somehow or other the Prince found out! which pricked Madame's balloon and caused the Prince a certain cooling off towards his protégé. But by now the youngster had learned all he needed to in Florence, and besides, he had secured a far more exciting invitation – to go to Rome to meet Maestro Corelli! There was so much he could learn of violin writing from him. And a year or two later, when he returned to Florence for the opening of 'Rodrigo', he found that Vittoria was not among the singers.

Tant mieux! Fate had smiled on him again. Ferdinand was so delighted with the opera that he presented the young composer with a hundred sequins and a costly service of plate. Having no need of it, for by now he knew that he would never marry, he sent it home to his mother.

Chapter 15
My First Love

I was alone in a sweltering hot land and because I was so alone and far away, I did things I would not have dreamed of at home. So that when he came to me that day in the garden, I was his master, and he was mine.

Rome!

I must have said it aloud in my sleep because I woke up with tears streaming down my face.

Rome, my first love!

Empire of my childhood reading, whose epic dramas had conquered my heart long before I had even heard of opera. I was a son of the lowly Saxon plains, and no Hannibal crossing the Alps with his legions could have felt more elated than I, when – winding day after day up through the clouds – I stood at last at the very summit and looked out over a vast panorama of snow-capped peaks!

And finally…*Rome.*

I was twenty-two. I was the greatest organist ever to have visited Rome, and I was intoxicated by this new world.

How many days did I gaze at Bernini's Baldacchino, drinking in its beauties? Its sculpted golden rays streaming from St Peter's throne right up to heaven, the painted ceiling of the Gesu with its saints flying out in all directions? And for the first time I saw, or rather felt, the livid blackness of chiaroscuro against a backdrop of blinding Roman light.

And in the afternoons, walking in cool galleries, I found the softer tints of succulent flesh, curving arms and muscular legs of veined marble, the warrior's hand fingering his weapon with the lightest touch.

The first few weeks I hardly slept.

And when I'd eaten and drunk my fill of these glories, I was more than ready for the hunt and I drew my bow: my quarry, three red-eyed, red-robed cardinals, Colonna, Pamphili, Ottoboni.

In the roof of San Giovanni Laterano, I improvised on the organ in such a fashion that they asked themselves in whispers if it was the devil playing. Knowingly, with stealthy calculation, I showered cascades of silver notes fluttering down on their upturned faces, I caused rows of invisible buglers to stand and blow their golden notes to the sky…and finally I shook the very columns like Our Lord in His righteous anger with such diabolical Saxon invention as held their buttocks rigid on the cold marble even as my flame melted their bowels!

Such power in my young hands.

How easy then, to get myself invited to Ottoboni's concert parties at the Palazzo della Cancelleria with its flambeaux flaming in the black waters of the Tiber. The evenings always ended in a five-course banquet of roast quail, guinea hen, sucking pig, the choicest wines and desserts, fostering in me a spirit of indulgence which has plagued me for a lifetime. Indulgence, yes – But only in that way. For the rest, *disgust!*

It was known – it was laughed about in Rome – that His Eminence had fathered sixty or seventy children, and had pictures of his mistresses, including his own daughters, dressed up as saints and hanging on his bedroom wall to arouse his passions. And this was Mother Church, to which these sly-faced, scarlet-robed sons of luxury would have me convert!

It was Ottoboni, of course, who conceived the duel between me and the virtuoso Domenico Scarlatti on the keyboards. Ach, how thrilling for this ageing *beast* to have two such handsome and gifted youths working up a sweat as we strove to dominate each other!

Domenico excelled at the harpsichord, having been brought up in the favoured Italian style, but of course my triumph on the organ was inevitable. My opponent, at the end of the performance, was pale and shaking. I'm told that ever since then, whenever my name was mentioned, he would cross himself, and I have some reason to believe it was true: as I toured around Italy giving organ recitals, I sometimes fancied that I saw him, wide-eyed and tearful in the audience.

And there was that night before the Carnevale, when I sat alone, demi-masked, playing the clavichord in a little music room that was so hot and so steeped in the melt of honey-candles that I almost swooned.

Was it *he*, wearing a unicorn's head, who came, and knelt hotly at my feet, and touched my arm?

But it was His Eminence Cardinal Pamphili who clapped the loudest whenever one of my cantatas was performed; he who presented me with a shamelessly flattering (some would say suggestive) Ode to myself comparing me favourably with Orpheus, which I was of course obliged to set to music. *Orpheus*, it went, *was able to attract birds, wild beasts, trees, and rocks, but couldn't make them sing; so how much greater are you who have been able to force me into song after I had hung up my plectrum on a dry tree where it lay motionless.*

Hung up *his plectrum*? A dry tree where *it lay motionless*?

Believing me now to be ripe for his possession, this worthy Cardinal lured me with a commission to set his allegorical poem 'Il Trionfo del Tempo e della Verita', and to make the offer even more tempting, he invited me to join the Society of Arcadians, a group of artists who worshipped all forms of classical beauty. So, as the Roman summer approached and all Rome melted away to the countryside, I accompanied Pamphili and the other Arcadians to the grounds of a country house. It was there, as the long light evenings emptied their sweetness, that painters, poets, philosophers and musicians lay on the grass, their arms entwined in the lengthening shadows under the myrtle trees; their alabaster bodies so languorous after bathing together that they scarcely knew where they themselves ended and their secret selves began.

DUETTO RECIT. ACCOMPAGNATO

'Of what are you thinking, Orfeo?'

'Of your 'Trionfo', Eminence, I think of nothing else.'

'Ah, our little drama. I have tried in my poem to show how very foolish Beauty is when she turns away from the mirror of Time and Truth to enjoy the pleasures of the moment. But, you know, Orfeo, when I look at the lovely male form, I can't find it in my heart to blame her. Wouldn't you agree?'

'The great poets have shown us that, sir. Perhaps there has never been a love like that of Achilles and Patroclus, unless it was David and Jonathan.'

'Ah, Orfeo, are we not blessed here in this place of reason and tranquillity? And no females shattering the peace with their damnable chatter!'

'How true, sir. My namesake Orpheus in the legend could withstand all dangers except the screeching of the Thracian women. Nonetheless I submit that females are indispensable, and not only for the purpose of reproduction. I do think the role of Beauty in our oratorio is better suited to the timbre of a lady soprano, than to a castrato *en femme.*'

'Orfeo, let's not think only of our work! The heart of my poem is not the end, where Truth and Disillusion triumph, but Beauty's lovely invocation of that happy band of youths, garlanded with roses and poppies, who, she believes, will never die away.'

'Although, sir, she imagines the Black Eminence as being one of sorrow...'

'With a smile on his lips, as a fair youth kills him. That's the sorrow I was writing of, Orfeo, the dying away of bliss. Do you not wish, as I do, to die in the very act of love? This is why at this very moment in the drama I want you to play the first sweet notes of your organ sonata, so that all who hear it will know of whom I speak when I say *his hands have wings, nay, his hands perform more than mortal feats.'*

Years later when I presented this work at Covent Garden, I changed the organ sonata to a violin sonata and obliterated any possible reference to myself in the libretto. For I knew very well that the beef-eating British would have subjected me to their mockery.

Chapter 16

A Beginning

As soon as my hands are on it, I know it's a Schnitger. Yes, Arp Schnitger or his son built this organ. Unless it's a Duytshot. What a piece of luck to find in this desolate place such a well-crafted instrument! Covered in dust and leaves but still, praise God, intact, and on the ground, not up in a loft. Someone has looked after it, has doubled the higher ranks, seven pipes on the lowest E-principal, seventeen on the highest.

I get Valentius to send to the village for the carpenter's lad who is persuaded to come and make some minor repairs to the pedals, providing Agnes is kept well out of the way. He and the villagers think her disfigurement means she's a witch – how unjust! Dirty, drunken, and stinking she may be, but she has a good heart, and it occurs to me that in different circumstances, with a coiffure arranged over her ear, she might have been thought quite pretty. She clearly likes it at meals when I smile her my thanks. But mankind is the devil's prey, ignorant and cruel. We are *nothing* till we are touched by the beauty of our Saviour.

That's why when I return the next day, before sitting down to my work I brush the dust off the great Bible which is still lying there on the lectern. My nose, which for days has smelled nothing but damp stone walls and the reek of Agnes and her cooking, is excited by a subtle memory of incense in its bindings.

The chapel is silent in the way silence should be, with the singing of thrushes and chaffinches in the greenery outside filling the space. The only light comes from a pool of green at the door, and whirling motes of dust descending from the high windows.

For some minutes I stand praying with the precious Book under my hands.

Should I try to read?

Gently I turn a gossamer-thin page.

The script dances before my eyes.

But it doesn't matter, because Father taught me to love the Book so well, I can listen to almost all of it in my head.

I know that my Redeemer liveth.

The text that always comes to me first.

We carved it on my sister Dorothea's tomb, and I want it inscribed on mine when the time comes. How happy was I when Jennens chose that resounding proclamation of faith to be the quiet, understated climax of 'Messiah', which alone could bring about the miracle of "*And with His stripes we are healed*".

And how happy when he moved from Job's unshakeable, *I know, I know*, into Paul's vision of the risen Christ, the Prophecy rising unstoppably into the Fulfilment – calling forth my own masterstroke, the "I know" expressed by me as an Ascending Fourth and becoming my triumphal motif throughout the work!

Job. I would have liked to make an oratorio for him. So much suffering, so much endurance.

But now, I think as I heave myself onto the stool, it's time for me to consider a far lesser Judge, Jephtha. I feel some uncertainties rise. And quite suddenly I find myself longing for tobacco! It's odd, I'd forgotten about my long-stemmed pipe, but now that some concentration is called for, my teeth hunger to bite and chew on the stem, and I desire the smoky whiff of black shag, the bubble of fire as it takes hold and powers though my veins!

Can I love Jephtha as I once loved Saul, Solomon, and Samson?

He makes a vow with terrible consequences. He causes an innocent child to suffer. And it's not just his destiny, it's the story of a people, Israel, the forefathers of Our Precious Saviour.

So…is it a work of tragedy? Or of ultimate victory?

I become aware that for some minutes now I've been pedalling and playing some chords. It's the ache in my knees that makes me stop pedalling, but my hands carry on silently, just as at home on my little night organ when I play silently so as not to wake the neighbours. Strange how I'm already at home in my big red house-robe and slippers, and also here in this ruined chapel in my cassock and sandals. I move effortlessly in and out.

So, is the issue really Jephtha's character, his pride? Forced by the Israelites into exile because he was illegitimate. Then the tribe beg him to forgive them, to come back and lead their armies against the Ammonite. He accepts the challenge in the name of Virtue but…it's more like condescension. He's still hurt, determined to prove he was right, and they were wrong…

And already I have his hurt, his swagger, a dotted rhythm that *seems* heroic but *sounds* dangerous:

> VIR*tue my soul shall still embrace,*
>
> *GOODness shall MAKE me GREAT!*

I'm beginning to know this man. It seems we have much in common.

Chapter 17
Marriage Plans

'This is all wrong,' says Valentius, eyeing with disapproval the assorted dishes that Agnes is preparing, 'He's in recovery, he should be on a light diet.'

'I know what he likes better than you,' she growls, 'leave it alone.'

'What's this? Stuffed sheep's heart, stewed eels, and what's this? A mulberry cheese.'

'And a nice marrowbone sauce for his bread, plenty of it, and try and stop me!'

'But you're going to kill him like this!'

'No, I ain't. He likes my cooking, he had second and third helpings. I'm making him strong again, then he can marry me.'

'"Marry you?" For heaven's sake, Agnes, he was a starving animal!'

'You can marry us, you wears the robe.'

'I'm not a priest, as well you know. The very idea.'

'It's not me wants to kill him, it's you! I know what you gives him and I know why.'

Valentius feels his heart beating uncomfortably fast. He looks at her. She has turned towards the window and is vigorously stuffing some dead marigolds into a broken jug.

'Make him drink and talk in his sleep so as you can get money for it. Like you did the others. When he marries me, he'll be master here. And I'll be Queen. The Queen of Heaven!'

'The herbs are part of his treatment. You wouldn't understand.'

'O I understand, I'm like a dog, I hear everything.'

The patient is told he might walk up the stairs, to take it slowly and that it will be good exercise. He has asked the hermit to trim his beard, hair, and nails, though he snorted with impatience while it was being done; he's getting restless downstairs. He must at all costs be kept away from Agnes! She's obsessed with him, more so than with the others and her accusations are getting wilder, so that despite the usual prohibition, sooner or later she will speak slanderously to him of her master.

Valentius decides to conduct a small experiment. He will invite the man to make free use of the study, then leave a book open on the desk and observe him through the spyhole in the wall which the late Abbot had installed for his own dubious use. The book will be one of Newton's, which he has lost no time in looking up in Father Anthony's library.

94

Of course, the patient was right, Newton did indeed argue that the laws of nature are nothing but the discoverable rules of God "who does uphold, direct, dispose and govern all creatures, creations and things".

> *But why,* Valentius writes later in his book, *does Newton attribute to God a human activity like Governing? Is this not again to fall into the notion, the arrogant notion, that we humans are the pivot of the universe, that our mode of life alone reflects whatever we are pleased to call Divinity?*

He hears a clumping up the stairs, a pausing and panting every few steps. Then from his position at the spyhole he watches the man hobble in and make his way to the deep bay window where he stands for some time shading his eyes with his hand surveying the summer sky and the forested horizon. It's impossible to tell from his face if he resents his incarceration and is plotting his escape, or if he's reconciled to surveying the world from this vantage point.

Then he turns round to the desk, sees the bowl of ink powder, the quiver of pigeon quills, a leather-bound book lying open. He hobbles over to the desk, picks up the book, lifts it close to his face, stares at it, puts it down. And the hermit sees, not to his surprise, that the man is crying.

Chapter 18

Messiah: A Private Miracle

'Here is something, perhaps,' announces Dr Morell, his bony finger holding open a certain page. 'It might be worth following up: *The Prince Stadholder dined on Wednesday last at the estate of Count Wassnauer-Oppdam.*'

I've heard that name before,' says Mary. 'Oh yes, the Pleasure Gardens with the stone statues. My brother saw them and said they're amazingly lifelike.'

'It says here,' continues Morell, '*On leaving the Count, His Serene Highness set out for Tulpenburg, a country seat near Amsterdam, and from thence to Soesdyke to meet with the Princess Royal.*'

'The Princess Royal. Of course! She's away in Holland visiting her husband's family. And of all the King's children she was Mr Handel's favourite pupil. Naturally, she'd invite her old music master to break his journey and travel onward with them! So all we have to do…Gentlemen, will you please go to Dr Delany's library and find his maps of the Low

Countries. Surely, we can find those two estates, or towns, or whatever they are.'

'Tulpenburg and Soesdyke, ma'am.'

'Thank you, Dr Morell. And when you've found them, I shall ring for dinner. Shall we say three o'clock?'

*

'Think of it, Anne, the Princess of Orange, our own Princess Royal! If he's travelling in her entourage, he'll be enjoying every comfort. She loves him even as we do and is a model of duty, likely to be made Regent of the Netherlands on Orange's death. What else but duty could have induced her to marry him, with his hideous humpback? She's said to have told her father *I would marry him even if he were a baboon.* Oh sister, why do we women have to endure these degradations? I almost wept for pity to see how pregnancies have wasted her, she being already so disfigured with pox pits, when she attended the London premiere of 'Messiah'. Oh Anne, do you not just die with impatience to hear 'Messiah' again? When he comes home, I shall entreat another performance! Here is Mr Smith returned from the library to fetch more candles, I shall break off here and ask him.'

'Another performance, ma'am? I think you know Mr Handel intended 'Messiah' for the Lenten season, to open our ears to the coming back to earth of Christ.'

'Of course I know that, Mr. Smith. But I don't think I can wait half a year till Lent. Consider the first part, the Nativity. Don't you think people would like to hear those joyful choruses at Christmastide?'

'Christmas, ma'am? Mr Handel would never consent. It would imply that Our Saviour's birth is more important than His Redemption of mankind. I pray you will never suggest it!'

He bows and hurries out with the candles. No doubt Morell is growing impatient for his dinner. If he was not on such an important errand, she would have stopped him and described how this greatest of oratorios had performed a miracle in her own life, in Patrick's life. It had, quite literally, healed Patrick – indeed he would not have married her, but for the chance of hearing 'Messiah'!

Given her feverish state of mind, she is not at all surprised to see Patrick himself, in his preacher's black coat and hat, floating through the wall of the parlour.

'Doctor D!' she cries, feeling the warmth of him surround her. He takes her hands between his own, they look into each other's eyes and smile.

Then he pulls her gently down to the settee, as of old, and settling among the cushions, she rests her head on his shoulder.

'What I did at the premiere,' he whispers, 'sure it was a wild thing I did, but consider now: my first wife had died only a short while before, and I didn't know that one day with you, my pet, I'd find an even deeper love. I was still in the agony of my loss when some kind friends in Dublin took me to the Fishamble Hall to hear Mr Handel's new oratorio. I arrived there in a condition of utter loneliness, I couldn't eat, sleep, or pray, I was cut off even from God. But from the very first notes of this sublime work, the light began to break into my darkness. The music was like a friend; it bade me Be Comforted, and I was comforted, it bade me Be Uplifted, and I was uplifted to the very gates of heaven! The glory of the Lord shone round about me.'

'A miracle!' murmurs Mary. She nestles her nose into his hair, and he strokes her cheek, as they had done in this room the night before he went to Dublin.

'So, thanks to Mr Handel, I found God again, and I realised He had never forsaken me.'

'And not only you, my love; many others have found Him through 'Messiah', even those, I believe, who have no religion.'

'And then, in the second part of the piece, *she* enters. Mrs Cibber in a long black opera gown singing, *He was Despised.*'

'And her hair hanging loose and alluring about her shoulders, no doubt, the little drama queen!'

'Now, Mrs D! A trifle waspish.'

'Dr D, she never let him forget she was a helpless girl, a third his age. She had him closeted with her in the music room, hour after hour "to teach her the music one phrase at a time " – look, Susannah Cibber was an actress. If she could learn roles like Perdita, Desdemona, Ophelia, she could have taught herself to read music!'

'The fact is, Mrs D, he loved her. We know, don't we, that everyone needs someone to love. Something in her, the aching melancholy of her voice, the pleading in those big dark eyes, must have touched the core of his being.'

'But did *she* love *him*? After all, she married someone else.'

'Her misfortune, my dear, to wed that rogue Theophilus. How would you feel if I did to you what he did to her? That to pay off my debts, I procured you a wealthy lover, yes *procured*, and then set the three of us up in a house together so I could blackmail your lover? That's what her husband did to her. Do you blame her for looking to Mr Handel for something purer, more beautiful? And,' he continues, seeking to draw his wife's fire off the gentle Susannah, 'Tis said the reason she couldn't bear a healthy child was because that blackguard gave her the pox.'

'O WHY MUST WOMEN ENDURE SUCH THINGS! I wouldn't let you treat me so, you old goat!' she cries and pretends to bite Patrick's ear, which makes him chortle goatishly.

'Wife, you have the strength of ten men and don't I love you for it! But for shame, can't you find it in your heart to pity Susannah? A great power on the stage, but at home abused and degraded. And if that wasn't enough, the brazen hypocrite of a husband drags her through the law courts and brands her publicly an adulteress, just to screw the damages out of her.'

'Which hurt Mr Handel as much as she! *He* had to see the cartoons of her in the newspapers, half-naked, bedding her lover with the husband looking on – *he* had to hear the guffawing in the coffee houses.'

'The English called her a whore, they lambasted her for playing the virtuous heroine on the stage and taking a lover in real life. But sure, didn't your Mr Handel fool them all? Fetching her to Dublin to sing in his *sacred* oratorio, making her into Mary Magdalene, as if 'twas only herself could give voice to Our Lord's disgrace. So, there was I in Fishamble Hall, and this poor little creature pouring out Christ's sufferings with all the sorrow in her heart, and 'twas so affecting, I couldn't help myself, I jumps to my feet and cries out for all to hear, *Woman, for this all thy sins are forgiven thee*!'

Mary sits up and glares at the cushion which is her spouse. She's still not quite sure how she feels about Susannah.

'And because you did that, the audience forgave her. And because of that, society took her back into favour – and now she's the highest paid actress in the land and has neither time nor inclination to sing for Mr Handel. So, if it's true he loved her, he's lost his muse and his dream, thanks to you. Thank God *som*e of us are loyal!'

'Well, Mrs D,' he replies manfully pulling her back into his embrace, 'you are chief among his women. But don't be giving your heart away to him just because you and I are apart for a few weeks. You're mine, and I'll prove it to you!'

When Lizzie summons them to dinner at three o'clock, she observes that they all, and especially perhaps her mistress, look weary but satisfied. The two gentlemen are relieved that their searches have unearthed the likeliest route taken by the royal party; and it only remains to verify that Mr Handel is travelling with them.

Chapter 19

Lento, Agitato

I shall go mad here!

I've lost count of the days. I pray morning and night but which day, which night?

He says I need more rest, more quiet. More dreaming.

Or remembering. I can no longer tell.

*

Why did you do it, Meinherr? You dared to use secular cantatas, *love-songs*, for the tune of *For unto us a Child is Born* and other sacred choruses – can that be right? Well, WHO DOESN'T? Herr Bach, whose 'Weinachts-Oratorium' I heard in Leipzig, uses three of his own secular cantatas in that work and has anyone taken *him* to task? DOES HERR BACH GET ACCUSED OF LAZINESS? Not to mention the borrowings *from* me. Before I even got to England, I found that scoundrel Walsh had published some airs from my 'Rodrigo' without permission and the soprano Francesca Vanini had inserted one of them, with different words, into a comic opera!

In fairness to Morell, this time he's drawn much clearer characters.

Jephtha, so rash in striking a bargain with Jehovah, but felled by his daughter's cheerful resignation. Utterly humbled. Broken. *Deeper and deeper still, thy goodness, child, pierceth a father's bleeding heart.* What Chorus can follow that, what all-consuming outburst of despair?

Is it despair?

Storge, a mother wracked with fears for the child she will lose, but fiercely protecting, fiercely forgiving. Her arms open, her heart beating warm. Mother. MOTHER!

And Iphis, my sweet-natured girl who laughs and makes light of her fears, with no thought in her pretty head but in pleasing the men she loves.

A child, who will never be crushed by disillusion.

Her music must radiate pure joy.

Chapter 20

Susannah

I remember the joy, Lord. She was mine, though not in the way the world understands.

That first time was 1733, and she was as sweet and silly as my little sisters when I taught them to sing. She was wearing a pale blue gown and her dark eyes were fluttering. From my seat at the harpsichord, I watched her take an enormous breath, as professionals never do, which she tried to make last for the whole of the phrase *How lovely is the blooming fair, the blooming fair, the blooming fair, whose beauty virtue's laws refine...* which of course ended in an unladylike gasp.

> 'Think of singer and instrument,' I said, 'as two friends playing a game. One calls, and the other answers, one leads and the other follows. This is how the warrior Barak praises the beauty of the prophetess Deborah with the words *How lovely are the blooming fair*. Are you ready to try again?'

> 'I shall let down the whole oratorio!'

> 'It's all right, this afternoon belongs to you. For some reason I have nothing to do today.'

'But I can't sustain the long note on *refine.*'

'No matter, I cover you at the end of the phrase, use this moment to take breath. And remember, we are two friends playing a game.'

She may well claim our softest care…for sure she almost seems divine.

'Good. This is sounding well.'

I got up and crossed over to her, showed her to a chair, sat down opposite her.

Even then I was re-living the pleasure of her voice; it had a womanly fullness that was extraordinary in a girl of eighteen, and it throbbed with something deeper than warmth, a kind of a pulsating darkness that excited me beyond words! Already I knew she could express the greatest sadness in the world, and the greatest consolation. She was made for tragedy, but what could this child know of tragedy?

I saw the carafe of wine sitting there on the table, but I was trembling and forgot to offer it. She fanned herself and dabbed a perfumed handkerchief on her cheeks.

'You are patient with me, considering.'

'Considering my reputation with singers. The difference is, they always dispute, but you listen to me.'

'I would never dispute with you, sir.'

'You were afraid what I will say? Everyone knows I throw difficult singers out of the window.'

'I thought the tale about Madame Cuzzoni was invented! Did you really threaten to throw her out of the window?'

'Yes, may God forgive me. And should you displease me, it would be easier to carry you in my arms than Madame Cuzzoni.'

'You make it easy to learn. The words and your music fit so naturally together.'

I longed to hear her sing again but realised she needed a rest. She was playing juvenile parts in the theatre and the occasional role in light opera, but inside that little body she had a mellifluous, yearning contralto, and already I wanted it more than I had ever wanted a voice. The thought came to me that, *for her*, I might one day compose more movingly in English than I could for my dazzling, infuriating, Italian divas– and who knew where this would take my art?

I picked up my Bible from the table and opened it where the marker lay in the Book of Judges.

'Holy Scripture has many passages in praise of beautiful women. The story of Barak and Deborah is one of my favourites.'

'But the Bible is very severe on us women. It says that if our virtue is once lost, then our beauty is lost.'

'There are some women who, I believe, would never lose their beauty, no matter what they did.'

Did I say that? I heard someone say it, and I felt her eyes snatched away from mine. *How could I have said that?* She jumped to her feet, her gown billowed out and she started

107

walking about the room looking rapidly at the volumes lining my shelves.

'My word!' she cried, 'All these manuscripts! Are you in the music printing business?'

'The music editing business. I must continuously make changes to keep occupied the singers in my company, for I have to pay them whether they work or no. So these are the latest version of my operas. See, here is 'Alessandro', this is 'Tolomeo' with some notes inserted, and here I am working on my new piece, 'Orlando'. '

'Yes, this page is quite black with alterations.'

'Sometimes I wish I could not find so many ways to improve my work. Always the ideas come. I rush out of the house, go down the street and walk in Hyde Park, but still the musical ideas buzz round my head like, how do you say, a swarm of bees!'

'I know just what you mean!' she exclaimed, 'it's the same for me when I'm acting. I have to try out every word and gesture in a hundred ways, and even when I'm applauded, it only re-kindles my desire to – to be worthy of my gift, if I may use that word.'

This perfecting torment is something we shared, and part of the joy was knowing that she understood. It hurts me, Lord, when people say I'm a showman, that my continual operas and oratorios mean I'm only in it for the money.

They don't know what music is to me; they don't know that the wooden keys of my harpsichord are hollowed out with my practicing day and night. Music is my sanctuary from the wrongs of men, and the dullness, as it often is, of the solitary life. Nobody but one who loves music can hear, in the sad depths of a minor sequence, something wonderful that is cradled in its heart, that stirs, the major key that lives in it unseen, that suddenly bursts into the sky and blazes joyfully as through a stained-glass window, making the whole world bright and new!

And so I'll tell You about Hyde Park, Lord, and You'll know if it was real, or a dream.

I don't think many of my English works would have been written without that place. I used to walk down Brook Street with my stick, quite slowly, sometimes managing to recognise my neighbours as they greeted me. They pitied me because I was always alone, but I didn't need their company, in fact I didn't want it, as I was on my way to the greatest free concert on earth: trees rustling, cuckoos calling, herds of sheep bleating, nibbling the grass, whispers of leaves falling in their season.

It was a few years after the scandal that rocked our lives, which I pass over as the pain was unbearable. The only consolation in that nightmare is that when she came to me in Dublin for 'Messiah', by putting the words of Christ's suffering into her mouth, I could proclaim her innocence to the world. Yes, by her liaison with Sloper she had sinned, but only because that *SCHEISSLOCH* of a husband forced her to it!

I spent some days teaching her *He was Despised* for the premiere, which is still talked about in Dublin and which I will never forget: her lusciously sustained phrasing, the anguished cries *Despised! Rejected!* she made so beautiful, the B section when we suddenly raced away together to that wildly articulated *Shame and Spitting!* so powerful I almost stopped playing…

But by 1742 we were back in London, she had rid herself of the *Scheissloch* and settled down with Sloper, who couldn't marry her but, I will say, behaved with decency and devotion. My oratorio 'Samson' was in preparation and I'd created a new part for her, Micah, the hero's friend and adviser. It was a bigger role even than Dalilah which I'd given to the spirited soprano Kitty Clive, whose mixture of Irish and Cockney accent I found just as droll as the English found mine. Although I was not blind and never thought to face that calamity, Samson himself I felt closer to than any character I had ever set to music: a man chosen by God, but dragged downwards by his own weakness of the flesh. I was enthralled by Milton's Samson Agonistes, a man having his excuses stripped away one by one and finally, after confronting the truth, finding a new way of serving God and his people that he could never have imagined.

We went for a walk in Hyde Park. We were laughing over Kitty, who had just been to a rehearsal at my house and had thrown one of her tantrums when she found out that Susannah's part was bigger than hers. We sat down on a bench overlooking a little pond, and watched some boys sailing their toy boats: it was still a fine afternoon, I remember, but some clouds were reflected in the water, and after a while the children went away. I remarked how fortunate she was to have a child, her adorable little Mollie.

She said, 'You write wonderfully for Samson because you understand a man who is *separate to God*. Tell me, then, how can…Micah…help him?'

'By listening. By caring what happens to him, just as you do. You are trembling, Susannah.'

'It's growing cold. Look, everyone else has gone.'

'So, rest your head on my shoulder, it will keep you warm.'

'Now we can't even see each other, it's like being in the confessional.'

'In your Catholic church, yes. As a Protestant, I say the great sky is our church.'

'Let's not leave Samson any longer in his despair.'

'He brought it on himself, by giving his heart away. The ones he loved always wanted his powers, but never himself.'

'Are you speaking of the Woman of Timna, or Dalilah?'

'All women. He was born to greatness, but he was weak, unworthy.'

'But God found him worthy. Whatever sins we fall into, His mercy is boundless. You taught me that, George, when I stumbled and fell.'

'So when he longs only for death and believes his evils are hopeless, it is Micah who begs God to return to Samson and renew his spirit. And again, it is Micah who announces the arrival of the treacherous Dalilah,

111

as Milton writes, *sailing like a stately ship with all her streamers waving in the wind.*'

'What a marvellous description! I can just see Kitty Clive in full sail with all her streamers waving!'

'Ach, you remind me, I have to go and see that *screeching bird* and smooth down her feathers.'

'That's Kitty to the life! How does she behave when Samson confronts her with her treachery?'

'Well, first of all, she weeps counterfeit tears.'

Susannah burst into exaggerated stage weeping, which made me laugh.

'And then she swears the fault was not on her side.'

'Ow, I am innocent! I ain't never done nuffin' wrong!'

'Mrs Cibber! With this talent for mimicry your serious admirers would be quite shocked!'

'I know for a fact that she does an appalling imitation of me.'

'But she finds that all her amorous cooing is to no avail.'

'Ow sweetheart! Tis only you wot I have ever loved!'

'Get thee hence, temptress!'

'Kiss me to show there is no ill-will!'

'Go forth or I will smite thee!'

'Kiss me, O kiss these dainty rose-red lips!'

O Susannah! I cried, a few moments later, I forgot myself! Yes, she said, blushing, looking away from me, we were just, well, we were just *playing*. We are both performers, we have been all our lives. But please, Susannah – No, my dear, she said, it would only bring unhappiness to those I love. And this isn't the story that's been written. Let's go back to town, it's got so dark, it could rain at any moment. Tell me, as we go, the rest of the story. Of Samson.

I told her that he renews his vow to God, and his power returns. And he realises that the sensual pleasures that he still enjoys are mere distractions. He must conserve all his strength for the task God requires of him. Yet he can only accomplish it…by giving up his life.

A sudden downpour forced us to take shelter in a pavilion.

We stood in there a few minutes, protecting each other from the rain. She saw the wet drops on my face and understood that it was not rain.

Chapter 21
The Letter

A few days later Valentius was writing at the desk in his study when Agnes clumped into the room; he was preoccupied with writing and only became aware of her when she threw a letter down in front of him.

The shock of receiving a communication from the outside world was so great that he did not at first notice she had changed her hessian tunic for a gown crudely cut from blue cloth and had forced her unruly hair into thick grey braids that stuck out absurdly on one side over the bulge of her ear.

'Who brought this?'

'Man on a horse.'

It was addressed to the Father Superior of the Order and sealed with a stamp from an office in the City of Haarlem. He opened and read it quickly, then he sighed and read it again, examined the seal on the envelope, put it down on the desk.

'This is important. It's about him. Where is he, anyway?'

'Chapel. He's always in the fucking chapel!'

'Be quiet. I have to think. They're trying to find him, his friends in London.'

'Eh?'

'London. Here!'

Valentius jabbed with his finger at a small terrestrial globe that stood on its curved stand on the desk. Agnes watched as he spun it round. She understood well enough that he was agitated about this spinning, coloured ball.

'It's from someone who used to know Father Anthony, to find out if we have any news of our patient. Agents of the Prince Stadholder are trying to trace him. It means we don't have much time. He'll be leaving…why, Agnes, what's the matter?'

It was shocking, Agnes's blotched and bloated face crumpling into tears, so that more than ever she resembled a gargoyle from hell. Red tears oozed from her eyes, chased each other down her cheeks and stained her bodice. She flailed her arms and squealed like a stuck pig.

'Don't send him away! No, no, no!'

'You're wrong, I want him to stay.'

'Then why won't you let me have him? I'll make him happy!'

'If I thought for one moment you could, or that he could make you happy—'

'He wants a wife! I know he does, he likes my cooking!'

'Look, he's a big man, he was starving—'

'You won't give him me – so I'll take what *you* want!'

She snatched up the letter, tore it into shreds, hurled the pieces up in the air, then grabbed the globe and threw it violently against the wall where it smashed into fragments. Valentius watched her sadly, his heart ached. She didn't know how insignificant those items were in comparison to the despair she was feeling. He almost wished she would attack him instead, because for so many reasons he deserved it.

'Let me have him.'

'He's a sick man, he isn't right in the head!'

'Just one night with him, then! One good poke of his cock up my cunt—'

'Stop this foul language at once!'

She rounded on him triumphantly.

'Father Anthony learned it me so you can't say nothing!'

She wound her braids round her engorged ear and hoisted it up with her hair onto her head, creating a monstrous crown. She stared appreciatively at the wall as if looking in a mirror.

'I'll be a bride. And soon I'll be Queen.'

'Agnes, will you listen to me—'

'No, you listen. It's *him*!'

From far away came the faint sound of an organ. Agnes let her hands drop so that the flesh-and-hair crown collapsed on her shoulders.

'That's my husband to be. He don't need you no more. He's master here now.'

She smiled beatifically and swept out of the room. The organ music continued distantly, growing in complexity. Valentius continued to sit, without moving.

But much later, by candlelight, he wrote his last entry:

All I have done in this place is to offer mankind an escape from the illusion of Grace, that we might find our true inheritance. For this, I deserve death.

Chapter 22
The Lady Smiles

At the foot of the stairs Agnes looked at the Smiling Lady and had a beautiful surprise.

There was no stabbing pain in her heart. Instead, a warm moist feeling had opened up in her belly which was making her want and want and *want* to stroke the softness of the baby's cheek and smell his just-born baby smell. Oh, how wonderful – how wonderful – to carry a new life in your womb, to feel him thrust his way into the world, to cradle him in your arms and smile down on his clumsy kicking in a kind of rapture, just as the Smiling Lady is doing – because you have created another being who is also you!

Agnes began to sob as only barren women can, tears of humiliation coursing down her neck, soaking the queenly bodice through to her breasts. She knew what Father Anthony and the Brothers, for all their learning, had never known, that it's not just the lady in the picture who is queen of heaven. Every mother is a queen, every baby is her saviour. Agnes knew this without having the words to know it.

And she knew, too, it was Father Anthony's terrible thrusting rod that had given her these itching foul-smelling juices which oozed from her body so that no healthy baby could live in her, foul yellow juices that oozed and offended her, sometimes streaked with blood, so that when the mood was upon her she itched herself into demonic ecstasy, rejoicing in the pain, a smell so vile that the only way she could disguise it was to fill her body up to overflowing with thick sweet ale and spirits.

But this time her shame turned to tears of joy. For she heard the clunk of the stick and the heavy footsteps of her King crossing the courtyard.

She knew what he was going to do. He was going to climb the stairs, go into the study, and ask Brother Valentius for her hand in marriage.

She must not lose a moment of this, the best day of her life! *She must hear him asking for her hand.* She would creep up the stairs after him to the annexe where she could both listen, and watch, through Father Anthony's spyhole.

Chapter 23

Sins of The Father

'Brother....er, Mister....I have recovered. Not just in the flesh, I mean that I have recovered my purpose and it's time for me to take the next step.'

Valentius noted that the man had changed back into his own clothes and was standing stiffly in them looking like a different person; but he made no answer.

'You've been unfailingly kind to me, and I thank you for that.'

The hermit raised his gaze with a great effort to look into the man's eyes. He saw that the yellowing tint was growing into a cloudiness and wondered how long it would take.

'What was that you were playing just now?'

'What was I playing? It was nothing, just improvisation. A seed pokes through, and sometimes it grows big enough for you to pick it up and hold it.'

'Sir,' said Valentius, sitting upright, 'You evade the question. You no longer answer truthfully because you believe people have stopped listening to you.'

'What CAN you mean, sir? How DARE you presume—'

'But I agree about taking the next step. I think we should name names. That fugue was composed by Quirinus van Blankenburg at The Hague in 1725. He claimed you stole it and published it in your Six Fugues of 1735.'

'That's a lie! I composed that subject in 1720, he tried to disguise it as his own! It always happens and I get blamed. Of course, you recognised me by my playing.'

'Indirectly, yes.'

'Or by listening to what a man cries out in his delirium? Is that a dignified way of finding out about your patients, *Doctor*?'

Now Valentius stood up and faced the bigger man's fury with the same unexpected resolve he had mustered once before.

'I met you years ago but wasn't sure at first. I could have addressed you by name, but it wouldn't have answered. The timing had to be yours.'

'And since we are naming names, who are *you*? Don't give me that B*rother Valentius.*'

'My name doesn't matter, I'm not famous like you. History will remember your works, not mine, and it's probably better that way.'

'Answer my questions! Why is Agnes living here with you?'

'Very well, if you must know, I brought her here at the request of Father Anthony. And it pains me to have to say it but...he abused her.'

'Oh God! NO, NO!'

'You asked for the truth. I mean that he pleasured himself with her.'

'O MERCIFUL GOD! BLESS AND HEAL THAT POOR CREATURE! In Your mercy, fold Your everlasting wings about her! AND YOU! – you knew of this Father Anthony, this *defilement*, and did NOTHING to stop it?'

Shaking with horror he stepped forward, raised the stick, and seemed about to strike the old white head bent before him, but something stayed his hand. He threw the stick on the desk, clasped one hand over the other and groaned.

'Should I have challenged Father Anthony?' the hermit asked in a trembling voice. 'You said yourself that fathers have Divine authority.'

'You twist my words! You twist everything!'

'Should I have defied the highest father of all – God – who, you say, ordained her suffering? Where were the everlasting wings when Father Anthony took her on his knee and pulled down her skirt—'

'STOP! STOP!'

Almost vomiting with disgust, the big man grabbed the stick again and hobbled menacingly round the desk to the smaller man, who retreated backwards stumbling over his feet.

'You are an apostate, you are Beelzebub! I order you in Jesu's name to come out of the body of this man—'

'Sir, I am not the devil because there is no such thing. I am no more or less holy than you are, sir.'

'You despise the church!'

'I don't despise it. I just don't think we need it.'

'WHAT?'

'All the churches in the world can't regulate the beastly acts a man commits in his heart. The world will only change when each of us throws aside the sanction of Tradition—'

'You're deranged!'

'—when we abandon tradition, search our own life and accept it as the beginning of a new future, as I have done and you are beginning to do, as part of the ever-changing whole. Once mankind realises it has no special significance, no apartness from creation, we can reclaim our true inheritance, *our communion with all things*—'

'Pride! Vanity! Human beings did not create this world, nor can they know God's purposes!'

'But they know enough to want to know more. And what of all those who strive for faith and cannot have it, *cannot* believe God's promises? Are they to be cast into oblivion? Are they to have no commerce with their inner spirit?'

This idea struck the big man with such force that he stopped in his advance and stood, stupefied, as the small man, only outwardly calm, took the stick from his hands. Each of them stood, shaking, not seeing each other, in the light of the bay window.

'Sir, you had better know this: I'm no better than Father Anthony. My crimes are different but no less momentous. I told you I was a businessman. I travelled the courts of Europe supplying all their little luxuries, silks, perfumes, peacock's tongues, whips for their brothels, opium for their orgies. I knew the peccadilloes of all the nobility and so powerful was this knowledge, none of them dared offend me. So I would get invited to their salons to feast on hand-fed swan stuffed with baby starlings, and watch plays, operas, harpsichord recitals…'

'So you saw me play at some great house. What of it?'

'Look at your hands, sir, the tools of your trade. Yes, take a good look at them. How soft and white they are, the hands of a gentleman. Who made it possible to keep those fingers soft and white, so they need do nothing but play? Who skinned their own hands red and raw starching your lace so you'd look pretty when you sat in the grand salon and entertained a prince? Why, servants, of course! In London, Paris or Rome, my best-selling line. I bought the poor and sold them to the rich.'

'You suggest *I* am culpable because like everyone else, I have need of servants? But it was YOU who brought Agnes here to gratify the whims of a degenerate monk!'

'For a price. A very high price. It cost Agnes her reason. It cost me my livelihood. I had bought and sold unfortunates all my life but had never seen the results, I simply bought and sold. But this time I saw what happened, and I couldn't go on with my trade after that.'

'Does she know it was you who brought her here?'

'No, she knows nothing except that I protect her from the villagers.'

'So by protecting her here, you hope the great God – in whom you don't believe – will forgive you!'

Valentius, exhausted after unburdening his guilt, sank down on his chair. He handed the stick to the patient, who leaned on it heavily.

'No, nor do I seek forgiveness. That's another quarrel I have with the Christian faith. Pain is natural, it can't be nullified by placing your trust in someone or something better than yourself.'

The patient laid the stick down on the desk, turned round and stood squarely on his own two feet before his companion, addressing him in a quiet voice that was all the more powerful for being quiet.

'You're mistaken, sir. Pain may be natural, but so is praise. I was moved to compose by the desire to praise, to play my part in Creation. Listen, my brother, to the harmony that is all around us and ask yourself from whence it comes. You hear it too; I know that you do. To whom can we express our gratitude for this beauty, for life itself, if not to God? How else can a man such as I, having neither wife nor child, give the tenderness in my heart I was born with, if not to God's children?'

Now it was Valentius' turn to bury his face in his hands. His voice was a rasping whisper like a man about to die.

'If only you were right. If only it was true.'

'Who told you that you had wronged Agnes?'

'Nobody told me. I just know.'

'It was your conscience, the voice of God.'

'But *which* God? Why the Christian Father of Mercy, and not the strict and vengeful Jahweh?'

'Because only thus can Good triumph over Evil.'

'What is Good? A good day for the blackbird is a bad day for the worm.'

'Did the monks teach you *nothing*? Jesus came to earth to fulfil God's love, to replace law with love!'

'Your God does not exist.'

The big man froze instantly. The small man uncovered his face and sat up. They regarded each other as a lion regards a snake, without understanding.

'You know that for a fact, do you?'

'Well, obviously I can't prove it, but I believe—'

'O, you *believe*! Your rejection of Divine Justice is founded on a *belief* – in NOTHING! You worship the void, just as Lucifer did.'

'I know there is human justice. I'm prepared to accept that.'

Chapter 24
The Triumph

The deaths of Valentius and Agnes, which were talked about for many years afterwards, caused little more than a ripple in the current of the village.

When Agnes' quivering ear heard the Chosen One ask for her hand in marriage and then demand it with rising passion, and when her master so quietly and cruelly denied him, she found to her horror that she was unable to cry out or move a muscle.

Even when the shouting died down to hissings, and then to nothing, even as she saw her Saviour pick up the stick and clump heavily down the stairs, it was as if a lifetime of frustrated impulses had settled on her like a shroud.

But when she unfroze for the last time, her actions were swift and deliberate.

*

The villagers, seeing their gifts on the doorstep were uncollected, broke into the hermitage and found Valentius lying on the floor of the study. He had been strangled with a length of blue cloth.

They also found a large man sprawled on a chair in the kitchen surrounded by partially eaten dishes of food. He had drunk an enormous quantity of spirits and was still semi-comatose when he was hoisted onto a hurdle and dragged by oxen to the village.

It was not for another three days, when a Bishop celebrated for purging witches arrived, that the women were allowed to go out to feed and milk the animals, and a hurriedly assembled militia in armour, gauntlets and holy texts went in search of Agnes.

They found her almost-naked body deep in the woodland, and rejoiced that it was still, just, alive; so that everyone, down to babes in arms, could witness the triumph of the Church over Satan as the hideously evil thing was immolated on a pyre.

Entre'acte

It is the evening of 28 September 1750, and Charles Burney is leaving Covent Garden Theatre with a man who was once his music teacher and is now, at the age of forty, a successful composer: Thomas Augustine Arne. They have been watching Arne's sister, the renowned Susannah Cibber, playing the role of Juliet, and as always, her performance has moved them both to tears.

Arne's eyes are wet with rage, Burney's with tenderness. He realises that it is only on stage, and in such a role as this, that Susannah is free from anxiety. Few of her adoring public realise how fragile she is because they have not studied her theatrical portraits as he has done. One painting shows her as Cordelia searching for Lear in the storm, reaching out and resting both hands on her attendant; in another she is the heroine in 'Venice Preserv'd' kneeling at Garrick's feet, begging to be spared his dagger, and even then, leaning on his arm and holding the hand of her oppressor as if upheld by his masculine power. She must always lean, always rest, on someone.

Thomas Arne is thinking that his sister has been made a fool of yet again, and that when he has a few drinks down him he may feel like calling that rogue Garrick out for a duel! Arne

130

can walk these streets whether blinded by fury or drink: he was born here in Covent Garden, an upholsterer's son who was not going to let humble beginnings blight his or his sister's chances.

The Great Square of Venus, as Covent Garden Piazza is known, is particularly noisy with revellers tonight, and the two men walk in silence past Haddock's celebrated Bagnio, so called because it offers exclusive services – such as *sweating, cupping, and bathing* – in addition to the more commonplace activities of bondage and flagellation. Immediately to its right is Mother Douglas's Brothel, and a few doors to its east, The Shakespeare's Head Tavern which Thomas Arne and Charles Burney enter, making at once for a private booth where they can drink and talk in peace.

'A great performance!' declares Burney, his eyes still aglow with the theatre's candlelight. At the age of twenty-four he is so much in love with Susannah that even a drink with her obnoxious brother is some comfort.

'A great performance that deserved a full house!' snarls Arne, his nose white with the foam in his tankard, 'which it would have had, if Garrick hadn't stolen half London for himself at Drury Lane. He knows my sister is still frail from her last childbirth and shouldn't even be playing Juliet in her condition. So what does he do? Adds to her stress by putting on his own 'Romeo and Juliet' – just for the joke of upstaging Susannah!'

'In fairness,' says Burney, 'he was rehearsing Romeo even before she left Drury Lane. But how foolish to quarrel with her and push her into the arms of the opposition. He'll never make up her loss.'

Burney's thoughts are not with Arne, who is invariably angry with somebody, but with Susannah whom he would have liked to fete in her dressing room with a bouquet of flowers. But he knows she will be too exhausted for company.

'She slaves for him all these years and now he *taunts* her with a rival production. It's these damned Wars of the Theatres, Charles! What is it about London that makes everyone stab each other in the back? NO DAMN LOYALTY!'

'Let Garrick play Romeo at Drury Lane; rest assure, the town will still say that Mrs Cibber is their Juliet. Nobody who has seen it will ever forget how she draws the poison from her lover's lips with that exquisitely gentle kiss, or how her fragile body shudders as she plunges the dagger into her heart and is transformed from flesh to spirit.'

Burney has seen all of Susannah's performances; and while he regrets the theatrical rivalry in which the great actress is caught up, it doesn't really touch him. For him Susannah is a goddess, and it pains him to be reminded that she is a flesh and blood woman who bears children. All he wants is to watch her onstage, if not acting then, even more incomparably – singing. The experience of hearing Susannah sing in Handel's oratorios is something which never leaves him, day or night.

With every mouthful of beer, he tries to swallow his deep resentment of Thomas Arne. How can this blackguard talk about *loyalty?* He'd like to ask Arne to explain his own *loyalty* to his sister. The way he sees it, the whole of Susannah's life she has been exploited by her family. It was Thomas and his father who got her to marry Theophilus, the reprobate son of impresario Colley Cibber – resulting in a sexual scandal that practically killed her! And then her in-laws the Cibbers pushed her into the role of Polly in 'The Beggars Opera' – a comic role for which she was manifestly unsuited, resulting in an unpleasant feud with the incumbent Polly, comedienne Kitty Clive. As if that wasn't enough, poor Susannah is now under fire from Peg Woffington, a self-made actress who is infuriated that Susannah's *divine helplessness* brings influential men like Garrick and Handel to her feet.

Burney knows that compared to them, he has nothing to offer her except adoration. *As yet.* Susannah is comfortably supported by her lover William Sloper, while Burney is a mere organist at St Dionis Backchurch at £30 a year. But already he has it in mind to enshrine Susannah and Handel in a "History of Music" which will confirm them as two of England's greatest geniuses. He has studied European music in depth and plans to pay generous tribute to the great J.S. Bach, who has taken the Sacred Art of Counterpoint to new heights; although Burney, a former chorister, privately believes Bach's music is less comfortable to sing because he treats his choristers as instrumentalists, plunging them time and again into unstoppable sequences of notes. Handel, by contrast, is always careful to give his choral singers time to collect their breath; he is, Burney believes, the unrivalled master of dramatic music, using space, silence, and echo with unforgettable effects.

Granted, Arne is the best of the home-grown composers, but he doesn't rate beside Handel. His patriotic air *Rule Britannia,* written to flatter his patron the Prince of Wales, has caught the public imagination. The old King has lost interest in rule, and even in browbeating his son, so the Prince is in the ascendant and for the present Arne is riding high – but that doesn't mean he's likely to put Susannah's interests before his own.

For the next step in Burney's plan, he must win Arne over to his thinking. But this will be difficult, given that the plan involves Handel.

> 'I think you know, Thomas, how deeply I admire her as an actress. I believe she would melt a heart of stone. But with her health so delicate, don't you think she should be protected from these thespian hyenas?'

> 'Susannah needs to be protected from *herself;* her judgement is that of a child. Luckily she has me to speak for her.'

> 'Quite so, quite so, your guidance is invaluable. So you could persuade her to leave the theatre for a time, leave all these squabbles behind her and resume her singing career.'

> 'Look, Charles,' says Arne, anticipating where this conversation is going, 'she cut her teeth on my music. I let the little thing sing in my operas because she was obsessed with the stage. But nowadays I compose for professional singers, it's what the public want of me.

Do you expect me to waste time on someone who can't read a note, just because she's my sister?'

'Of course, you're right,' says Burney hastily realising that some smoothing over is called for, 'the people who admire your 'Judgement of Paris', your 'Masque of Alfred', and your superb music for 'Comus' and all your Shakespearian settings.'

''Twelfth Night', 'The Merchant of Venice', 'The Tempest', 'Love's Labour's Lost',' interposed Arne.

'Yes, all those and much more have established you as a leading composer and mean that your time is greatly taken up. So then, if not your music, why not another's? Why should the world be deprived of one its truly great interpreters of song? When Mr Handel returns to London, just think what a sensation it would be, how it would enrage Garrick and his troupe of wildcats, if Susannah showed she was beyond their reach!'

'The *Saxon*? That vainglorious hog? Don't you think he's made enough money out of her?'

Arne sucks his cheeks into his long face: he is visibly bristling. He still sees Handel as The Usurper who got away it for decades because he was the King's favourite, him and his lousy crew of foreign fiddlers. But that's all changing now. Never mind the current craze for 'Messiah', which is, admittedly, a triumph – well, let it be his last triumph. Arne is sure that if he, as a Catholic, had been permitted to compose for the Anglican Church, he could have at least equalled 'Messiah'. He understands true Englishness as the Saxon never will, and he knows the English quickly tire of serious works. 'The Beggars Opera', that hilarious satire on politics and Italian music, has been a top draw for more than a decade and is still playing at a theatre in Covent Garden; some people have been to see it five or six times.

Given the change in public mood, Arne reckons his sister–who only does Tragedy and is a disaster at anything else – is lucky to be safely tucked up on her pedestal.

> 'Even the Saxon knew her voice was but a thread. Everyone failed to notice because her acting is so good and her stage presence so powerful. I admit the pig pulled off quite a trick with her, because he needed a famous name like hers to get his Oratorio off the ground, but frankly I doubt the public would pay nowadays to hear her sing.'

Burney pauses until the waiter has brought them a bottle of well-chilled Chablis and they have downed their first glassfuls, before replying to that point. He is aware that continuing to mention Handel will annoy Arne; but Burney is Susannah's acolyte and can never forego a chance to praise her singing.

> 'True, her voice without skilful management is a thread, but who else can penetrate the heart with feeling as she does? It's possible that when Mr Handel returns he may want her to sing again in 'Samson', it's such a favourite with the public. You wouldn't stand in her way, would you, Thomas?'

> *'When he returns?* What makes you think he will?'

'Well, for one thing, he hasn't disbanded his company. Signora Galli and Signora Frasi are ready to sing for him, as is John Beard.'

'You see? He's still obsessed with the Italians. He'd have signed up Farinelli if he could have afforded *him*. So he keeps on these worn-out scrubs like Galli and Frasi and tries to get his money's worth by putting them on with popular singers like Beard.'

'But doesn't Mr Beard's success rather prove Mr Handel is moving with the times? That he recognises the English preference for the tenor voice over the castrato, for dramatic expression over the decorative? Why else has he given that young man leading roles in all his operas and oratorios?'

'A fine tenor, I grant you, a powerful delivery. But he's canny. He's had the business sense to marry an Earl's daughter. Do you really think he'll nail his colours to a sinking ship?'

'A sinking ship?'

'Why do you think Handel skipped town? Only five years ago he was on the verge of bankruptcy. Over-reached himself and had to cancel the season. He must still owe hundreds to his subscribers.'

'But they refused to take back their money. There *is* such a thing as loyalty, Thomas. He deserved it too, after his service to the nation.'

'Service? Personal ambition, more like! He holds himself up as our leading composer with his 'Sacred

Oratorio' getting the Royal blessing, but Charles, even you must realise, change is in the air, the Prince's day is coming, and your Saxon has no future here. Look, he could live anywhere in Europe, they'd be glad to have him. I gather his friends have put some report in the press that he's been seriously injured in Holland – how convenient! He won't dare show his face again here.'

Burney puts down his half-empty glass; his cheeks are burning. He takes out a lace handkerchief and wipes his mouth. He has taken all he can of Thomas Arne.

'Regrettably, he was injured, but I'm told has recovered sufficiently well to perform on the organ for the Princess Royal. I believe he will come back, and if I know him at all, he will have music ready to open the new season.'

'Then he will do so without help from my sister. She is contracted to play for John Rich at Covent Garden and that's what she'll do, childbirth or not. Give it a few nights, the town will choose Rich's production over Garrick's, and you may as well know, I am joining my sister at Covent Garden, I signed with Rich last week. Did you mark how the audience were held by Juliet's Funeral scene? And my music for that scene, what did you think of the applause for *that*?'

'Oh…' says Burney faintly, 'I thought they were applauding the spectacle.'

Privately he thinks the interpolated Funeral Procession, with bell tolling, Capulet servants bearing live torches and flower girls strewing blossoms in the path of Juliet's bier, tasteless in the extreme. Arne's music he had barely noticed, as his interest in the play ended with Susannah's last exhalation of breath.

> 'The joke is,' continues Arne, 'Garrick is beside himself with fury, and has now put in a funeral procession of his own. He's even hired that hack Boyce to cobble some kind of music together!'

The eyes in the angular face are suddenly twinkling with merriment.

And this brings the discussion, which from Burney's point of view has been a failure, to an unexpectedly good-humoured close.

The infamous caricature of Handel as a Pig, entitled 'The Charming Brute' was published by the draughtsman Joseph Goupy in 1733 with the engraving printed in 1754. Goupy, formerly a close friend, claimed that he was invited to dine with Handel on the understanding that it would be 'plain and simple fare' and was outraged to discover Handel sitting by himself in another room feasting on rich food and fine wines. The banner under the seated figure of Handel reads 'I AM MYSELF ALONE'. The verses printed under the picture reads as follows:

'The Figure's odd, yet who would think
Within this Tunn of Meat and Drink
There dwells the Soul of Soft Desires
And all that HARMONY inspires.
Can contrast such as this be found
Upon the Globe's extensive Round.
There can – yon Hogshead is his Seat.
His sole Devotion is – to Eat.'

Chapter 25

Messiah: A Public Miracle

On 18th of April 1751, Anthony Ashley-Cooper, 4th Earl of Shaftesbury, is watching in excitement as the Chorus stand for the last time. He feels unspeakably blessed to be here, to be hearing the greatest music that he will ever hear.

The faces of the lords and ladies sitting around him are also shining with rapture. He knows these faces well: The Gainsboroughs of Exton in Rutland, where Mr Handel sometimes takes his holidays; his own Harris cousins, James, George, and Tom; the Granvilles, with Mary Granville Delany sitting next to her dear friend the Duchess of Portland. All of them were here for the inaugural performance of 'Messiah' last year, all have been counting the weeks till they could hear it again. They have adorned themselves in their finest jewels and lace, their rich silks and satins and powdered wigs, but from the very first chords of the grave overture, these adornments flew back into the shadows of the chapel to leave them naked and hungry for every note and every word. Shaftesbury supposes he must look *naked* too, because it's how he's feeling…like a child! His heart is wrung with gratitude to God for making the beautiful sacrifice of His Son to redeem the world, and to Handel for bringing it so wondrously to life.

'Messiah' has wrought its miracle. Some distinguished persons are openly weeping. In several of the choruses, peers of the realm have stood up and bowed their heads, as if in the Almighty Presence.

The Coram Chapel is hot with exhaled breath as every nook and cranny is crammed with bodies, gentlemen having again been requested to come without swords and ladies without hoops. A choir of thirty-two, little boy sopranos and altos at the front, tall men from the Chapel Royal at the back, are dressed in their dark suits with the white cassock over the top. Before them, the scarlet-jacketed orchestra; violins, violas, cellos, double basses shining with polished wood, great bassoons on their pedestals, gleaming horns and trumpets, and timpani. A magnificently bewigged Handel, resplendent at the harpsichord with his assistant at his side, raises his arm, fixes his gaze on the basses, then moves his hand upward and brings them in for the first, great long utterance of *"Amen…"*

Shaftesbury is already so uplifted by the Glory of the preceding choruses that he is struggling to contain his applause. How can this extraordinarily long fugal subject on *Amen* beset in so many ingenious ways? Forwards…backwards…inverted…counter-inverted, with the voice-parts taking it in turns to soar upwards and outwards, then plunging inwards and downwards with unstoppable mathematical power, the very Utterance of the Almighty!

In his own frenzy of delight, he barely takes in the clapping, cheering and calling, only dimly sees the soloists coming forward to take their bow, and now Handel comes forward. He is smiling with particular satisfaction because the new organ he donated – which to his fury was not ready for performance last year – he has finally been able to play, to the greater glory of God.

The music may have ended, but Handel is still at work: there are many generous benefactors who expect to be publicly acknowledged. He bows again and again to the Hospital Governors, the Bishops of Oxford, Gloucester, St Asaph's and St David's, the lords, ladies and gentlemen of this numerous, glittering audience. The little Coram children in their brown uniforms and white bonnets are being led out of the chapel, no doubt to resume their duties around the house and the farm, after the excitements of the morning.

Shaftesbury eventually pauses in his clapping and allows his gaze to fall on the magnificent picture over the altar, Casali's 'Offering of the Wise Men'. He knows that it was commissioned by Foundling Governor William Hogarth, who has himself painted the fine portrait of Captain Coram hanging in the main hall. What a remarkable stroke of fate it is, that today's performance has taken place not two months since the death of Coram. A fitting epitaph to that great man! He lived long enough to see the fruits of his own charity; and so, it's a relief to find, has Mr Handel despite that disturbing report about a coach accident in Holland.

Later, at a private reception at which Handel is effusively thanked, it is announced that a grand total of 785 tickets have been sold for this performance and that the extraordinary sum of £3000 has already been raised for the Foundlings.

Shaftesbury glows with pride in his friend. The Earl waits patiently in the queue for his private conversation.

> 'Well, my old Buck!' he exclaims, using the pet name reserved for Handel's inner circle, 'Even after these exertions, I never saw you looking so cool and well! We were told you'd been injured in Holland and confined to a hospice, but you seem to have taken no harm. What treatment did you have?'

> 'Oh, very little, my Lord,' replies Handel coolly, 'having escaped the wreckage with my life, the physician tried to finish me off with his nauseous herbal remedies and a regimen of starvation. But then there was a death at the hermitage, so I was found, and rescued, as you see.'

> 'God be praised that in this year of significant deaths, *you* have been spared!'

> 'Yes, indeed, my Lord. Whoever would have thought that in this year, Great Britain should lose the heir to the throne? And at the tender age of forty-four. I still cannot believe that a man in the prime of life should have suffered this fatal blow!'

> 'Your regret does you great credit. Prince Frederick was no friend to you.'

> 'His Highness was unfortunately used by my rivals against me. As a child he was my pupil and like his

sister the Princess Royal, he loved his lessons and was a skilled musician. I prefer to remember that.'

'We all hope that now the National Mourning has been observed, you will be able to resume your season of concerts.'

'Indeed we are. We are reviving 'Belshazzar', 'Esther', 'Judas Maccabeus', 'Alexander's Feast', 'Samson', 'Joshua', and I shall present the work I composed for 'Alceste' as a new piece called 'The Choice of Hercules'. You know, my Lord, I never waste good music while there is life in it.'

'Our old Buck is as resourceful as ever! I would take you for half your age. Where on earth do you get your vigour?'

'From my work. Always having a new and higher mountain to climb. Speaking of that, I will tell your Lordship confidentially that London will soon be hearing my latest piece, the oratorio of 'Jephtha'. I believe it will be a great work. That is, I hope it gives much pleasure and instruction.'

'It surely will,' replies Shaftesbury, realising that others are waiting and his turn is almost up, but he will say what he has come to say, 'though it would be hard to give greater pleasure and instruction than 'Messiah'. I never understood what The Glory of God meant till I heard these choruses. But now you've given it so triumphantly for a second year, I have no doubt 'Messiah' will become an annual British celebration. My honoured father I'm sure had just such a masterpiece in mind when he wrote his 'Characteristicks of Men, Manners and Opinions': he believed human beings are designed to appreciate order and harmony, and that through them, man can develop a true moral sense. Mr Handel, I have long meant to say this: your oratorios are a blessed gift to us, and to future generations. They bring the teachings of religion home to us through delightful music, and with an artistry never before attained. I will go as far as to say, you are helping to create the moral sensibility of this nation.'

'My Lord,' mutters Handel, overwhelmed, unable to find the words.

'And now, my dear Buck, I must give you up to the ladies. For we both know that ladies cannot be kept waiting,' he adds, seeing the formidable Mrs Delany standing and watching from a distance. 'And when your divine energy is in need of renewal, come and stay with us again in Dorset. The musicians of Wimborne St Giles long for your return and can never play your chamber pieces often enough.'

Chapter 26

A Sad Loss

If the Earl believes that Mrs Delany is impatient to be presented, he is mistaken. She is deliberately standing at the back so as to observe the composer, who is giving the well-wishers at the reception a performance at least equal to his direction of 'Messiah'.

She realises that the assistant who sat at the keyboard and turned the pages of Handel's score was there quite simply to create an illusion. Handel has performed the entire work from memory. He does not read it, because he cannot. It is doubtful he can see anything more than dim shapes with his one functioning eye.

Mary Delany has been concerned about Handel ever since his return from the continent, not merely on account of his failing sight; there is something much deeper going on, only visible to herself. She tried to draw him out about it in the weeks preceding the crisis in February, but he wouldn't speak of it even to her. Yet she was convinced it was troubling his very soul; and it may be doing so, even now.

In a lifetime of very public accomplishments, one of her private ones is her ability to lip-read. It is so useful at Court, where many a whispered aside has proved to be of interest. At present she is reflecting on the part of Shaftesbury's conversation relating to the death of Prince Frederick…and the words *Good Riddance* come immediately to mind.

But if Handel can speak so kindly of his old enemy, should she not think again?

After all, it's arguable that the Prince's character was ruined by his father, who quite openly loathed him – regarding him, correctly, as a figurehead for political opposition. A father who was as much a womaniser as his own father had been, and spent the time he should be ruling Britain, away in Hanover in the arms of his favourite mistress. It was mere chance that he happened to be in England (playing cards with another mistress) when the sensational news was brought to him of his son's death: Mary has it on good authority that the King merely remarked *Fritz ist tot* before continuing his hand. What paternal pig-ignorance! How could a son prosper with such a father?

Frederick, who allowed his friends to do everything possible to undermine the King's favourite composer, has been commemorated by Handel at Westminster Abbey in a finely wrought Funeral Anthem; and by the beef-eating British in a popular epigram:

> *Here lies poor Fred who was alive and is dead,*
>
> *Had it been his father I had much rather,*
>
> *Had it been his sister nobody would have missed her,*
>
> *Had it been his brother, still better than another,*

Had it been the whole generation, so much better for the nation,

But since it is Fred who was alive and is dead,

There is no more to be said!

It's this doggerel that Mary Delany remembers as she stands by the magnificent fireplace topped by marble busts and noble portraits, discreetly observing the smiling, bowing composer. How annoying that such a vulgarity should have come unbidden to a mind like hers which is so well-stocked with classical poetry! *It's odd*, she thinks, given the lofty artefacts all around us, that we retain trivia in our heads so easily.

But at least the untimely death of Fred means the backstabbing of the past forty years can't hurt Handel any more. The Prince's Party is in disarray, his son too young to rule. Augusta, Princess of Wales, has been made Regent in the event of the King's death – a woman determined to protect her son's interests but with scant ambitions of her own (so Mary's friends at Court have assured her). Nevertheless, Mary can hope that when the old King dies, Britain may have another chance with a woman at the helm – and Mary will be on hand to assist, if required.

She is watching Handel for any signs of exhaustion, or melancholy, under his practiced bonhomie. Why has he said nothing – *nothing* – of the events surrounding the accident last year? What did that visit to the continent do to him?

Did it stir up painful memories of a life he had left behind? And if it did – will this prevent him from finishing 'Jephtha'?

Will he *ever* complete his life's work?

Chapter 27
His Inner Voice

Mary knows all the stories he has told his two biographers, Mainwaring and Hawkins, and she has no doubt that his destiny to compose has been extraordinary.

Miraculous, really.

How he was brought up in a God-fearing house; how his childhood was partly pious but partly secret...an irresistible submission to his inner voice!

How his father, Barber-Surgeon to the Duke of Saxony, having higher ambitions for his son, refused to let him train for a musical career; how the boy smuggled a clavichord up to the attic and taught himself to play during the night when the family was asleep; how one day when his father went to visit the Duke, the child ran after the coach so that his father was obliged to take him to the castle; how the boy somehow found a keyboard and played on it, so impressing the Duke with evidence of his genius that he was given music lessons forthwith.

Mary has sometimes wondered if all these extraordinary adventures could be true.

But Handel is not in the habit of falsehood, and it shows how early in life he began to obey that inner voice. It's clear that he adored his father and regretted having to disobey him. He had given a promise that he would study law at the University of Halle, and he did...for one dispiriting year, before dropping out of university and giving himself entirely to music.

Of the mother he has only said she was a Pastor's daughter and that after being widowed she became totally blind; but from the way his face coloured when he spoke of her, Mary knows that his feelings for her run particularly deep. When the news reached him in London that she had died and already been buried, he shut himself up in the house in Brook Street for days, according to the servants, pacing the room and writing letters to his family in Halle with the tears streaming down his face.

He must have written to Johanna Frederica, his sister's girl. Long ago he had held that same child in her Christening robe at the cathedral font, vowed to protect her from the works of the devil, to teach her the ways of the Lord; a vow that his life in exile has forced him to break. When she married a distinguished doctor, he had two costly and perfect diamond rings especially set and sent them to the bridal pair. But he has missed her whole life.

Nevertheless, it seems to Mary that he has accepted the loss of his family. She concludes that what happened to him in February was not connected with Halle: it *must* have some connection with that period in Holland of which he will not speak. Because it was February, the dark mid-point between

the Nativity and the Ascension, when his combined darkness
of body and mind became impossible to disguise.

Chapter 28

A London Parlour

In the terraced house in Brook Street, as January blew to its icy close, Mary Delany and Dr Morell were waiting for Mr Handel to come out and greet them.

She observed, as so often before, that although this house must be the same dimensions as her own farther down the street, the rooms here seemed much too small for a man of Handel's girth, and he must frequently curse as his passing belly swept sheets of music off the tables. Considering he had amassed wealth with his success and invested it wisely, she thought the furnishings of the parlour were extraordinarily modest: nothing more than two card tables, a desk, and a few upright chairs. But there were some good paintings on the walls, a view of the Rhine, and a pair of magnificent Rembrandt portraits. Going to an auction house and bidding for fine pictures was the only leisure activity he indulged in, apart from evening games of cards at the Spas – *when* she could persuade him to visit a Spa for his health.

Lining the shelves were well-thumbed volumes of poetry in English, German, and Italian; countless musical scores and notebooks were stacked in cupboards round the hearth, where a fire of sea-coal burned smokily in the winter light. On the desk was a Lutheran Bible and prayer book, and the St James Bible lying open with a green fringed marker.

Mrs Delany and Dr Morell were sitting on high-backed rattan chairs, talking, and glancing intermittently at the door of the composing room, from which phrases were being played on the little house-organ to someone else, interspersed with sharp exclamations which suggested that the music was not going particularly well.

This mingled with sounds from the street outside: passing carts, carriages, cries of milk-girls and fish-women. It was a fast-expanding neighbourhood of elegant squares, favoured by nobles, wealthy merchants, and intellectuals like herself. The fine portico of the sparkling new St George's Church, Hanover Square, where she and Handel attended Divine Worship, was a fitting testament, she thought, to the Godliness of an Age ruled entirely by men. At this hour, she knew, the portico was being cleared of the beggars who congregated there, shivering and clutching their gin bottles: the Sexton's boy whose job this was, would be grumbling and cursing as he plied his brush among the slushy pools of brown snow and human detritus.

A shadow crossed her face: there was so much misery in this great city of hers, particularly for women. Across London, 730,000 people were going about their lives. It was a shocking fact that among the poor, one infant in every five would die before its second birthday, most of them addicted to gin like their mothers. Hogarth had painted a picture featuring that notorious, or, as Mary saw it, desperate mother, Judith Dufour, whose story spoke to the condition of these women: she had collected her two-year-old child from the workhouse and strangled him, selling his clothes for one shilling and fourpence to buy gin. Hogarth depicted her sprawling on some steps, blissfully unaware that she had just hurled her baby off her lap; and to the left of the picture he had shown the pawnbroker thriving, with a ready queue of customers. A few months later, when a new Gin Act had raised the tax on spirits so high they were uneconomical to supply, Mr Hogarth with his ever-topical brush painted Gin Lane's companion piece, Beer Street, where everyone is prospering except the pawnbroker who has shut up shop for lack of business.

Mary admired Hogarth's work, even though her own art was not in this satirical vein. She was entirely devoted to capturing the beauties of nature; it was a skill she was proud to share with Mr Handel in his pastoral works.

She glanced again at the composer's door, still resolutely shut.

Something is hurting him, she thought, *Something in his private life. I know it is. How can I get him to talk about it?*

She wondered if she should retire to her own house while he was so ferociously preoccupied with this new work. But despite the tedium of waiting, she persuaded herself to stay because she believed she was necessary to him at precisely this formative stage. He loved to play over his musical ideas and explain them to her, he valued her opinions more than anyone else's, so she would not disappoint him. She had admitted to Anne, however, that she felt concerned about her friend:

> 'Since last year, that mishap in Holland, something quite profound has changed. When we tracked him

down, he had gone to the Great Church of Deventer to play for Their Highnesses, and I am told he never played better. The injuries are healed but as to his treatment in that hospice he will say nothing, but it brings on a troubled look I have never seen before. To all appearances he is busy preparing a vast programme of revivals which would kill someone half his age and on top of all that he plans feverishly for 'Jephtha's' premiere but Anne, I fear so much, close reading weakens his eyes, he dictates to Mr Smith and flies into a passion if it is not quickly enough done, poor Mr Smith has a troubled look second only to Mr Handel's.'

Mary turned again to her companion who was sitting stiffly on the opposite chair, cracking his spindle fingers in a way that made her want to scream.

'He's been so shut up indoors, he won't have seen the announcement. Thomas Arne's son Michael is going to perform his father's organ concerto.'

'You think Mr Handel will spare the time, ma'am, to go and hear Thomas Arne's music? I'm not sure he rates it so highly.'

'He needs an outing, Dr Morell, he needs air and exercise. But the real point is, Michael's aunt is sure to attend the recital and I believe Mr Handel would like to see her again.'

'His aunt?'

'Mrs Cibber, Susannah Arne as was.'

157

'Ah yes, of course.'

'When Arne deserted his wife and child, she practically brought the boy up. She will surely find time to attend his debut – even though she finds no time nowadays to sing for Mr Handel.'

'It's a wonder to me that she ever did sing for him.'

'Yes, she was no Faustina or Cuzzoni. But you see, we women have learned to exploit the gifts nature has bestowed on us. She has a sensitive ear.'

Mary still had confused feelings about Susannah. She must admire a woman who, since her Disgrace, had managed to rise so far above all that disgusting male ribaldry that she had become the foremost tragedienne of the day. But Mary was troubled by her rival's unknown powers. It said much for her devotion to Handel that she was trying to set up a meeting between him and this ghost from his past; and for once, she hoped her efforts would fail.

There was a shout from the composing room, the door opened and Mr Smith emerged quickly, almost as if propelled from behind. He recovered his composure, went over to the visitors and made his bow.

'Mr Handel is coming now. He begs you will excuse him, ma'am, not having completed his toilette, but he has been working all night.'

The composer came striding out, smiling and bowing, resplendent as a cardinal in his huge red dressing-gown and Indian slippers; but though his eyes smiled, he was an unshaven, grey-faced cardinal, his grey hair was tousled and some of the buttons of his gown were undone. Through the half-open door Morell caught sight of the red turban lying under the organ and beside it, a half-empty bottle of brandy which he hoped Mrs Delany had not seen.

'Ah, my dear Mrs Delany!' said Handel kissing the hand that she extended towards him.

She smiled in return, recoiling slightly but managing to stifle a comment about the spirits and tobacco on his breath.

'No doubt you are wondering if 'Jephtha' makes progress?'

'Yes, of course I am, but if you are too busy—'

'Much, much too busy, but for you, dear friend, I will spare a few minutes to explain the piece. As you knew I would. And then, you will understand that Dr Morell and I have matters to discuss.'

He had no intention of explaining his process of composition. It would mean nothing to her that he was adapting themes from Carissimi and Galuppi and Habermann, and anyway he wasn't sure she would understand that more than ever he needed those borrowings to get fired off.

'Oh, how delightful! Though I really came to invite you to supper on Thursday and to come with us to hear Mr Arne's organ concerto.'

Madame, you are generosity itself, but why trouble to go out – even to hear the works of Thomas Arne – when the best music in town is right here in my little parlour? And where do you suppose he got the idea of an organ concerto, which England never heard of

159

till I invented it? Pray be seated, that's right. But before you go, Christoph, give me the news from your father.'

'Yes, sir,' replied the younger man, who had already given Handel the latest bulletin. 'He's going to put the notice for 'Belshazzar' in The Journal, and he's given me the corrected parts. I told you, sir, I've put them on the table.'

'Good. Now, wait here. I need to check them myself, so many mistakes I find these days. We're opening our Lenten season with 'Belshazzar', ' he said turning to Mary, ignoring Morell, 'and some other revivals to get the people through the doors and then we can sell them tickets for the new work. You see, *G.F. Händel* is very much back in business! Now,' he continued, 'since you and your gown are both comfortably settled, let us begin by considering our hero, Jephtha. In what way shall the music express his tragedy? We know that he begins the piece in triumph, giving heroic service to his country but then causes anguish by making a rash vow. In his first aria he sings *Goodness shall make me great! Goodness shall make me great!* Can you hear the swaggering in those rhythms? A man who believes in his rightness to the point where he courts disaster.'

Smith was thinking that he knew someone like this, who was quite possibly working himself to death, or at least to a serious breakdown in his health.

'My harmonic design is too complex to explain. Put simply, he veers all the time between G major and G minor, from obedience to God, to stubborn pride. Dr Morell here has created a whole family of characters who suffer as a result of his vow. You tell her, Morell, while I deal with these copies.'

He turned abruptly to the sheets lying on the table, held one up to his face and immediately started arguing with Smith about what was written there. Mary was greatly affronted but succeeded in disguising it. Never before had the composer treated her so openly as an interruption to his work! He must be deeply unsettled. She longed to get him to an oculist who could prescribe reading glasses; and she was worried because she had seen what the cook was preparing, fricassee of chicken, hare collops, calf's head pie, blancmange – richly unsuitable for his sedentary life. It was weeks since she had seen him walking down Brook Street to Hyde Park.

Morell was telling her again about Jephtha's family. It was the story of a girl cast as a happy, willing sacrifice, whose only purpose in the oratorio, as in life, was to fulfil the male's covenant with Jehovah; a mother clinging passionately to both husband and daughter, but thrown aside, a Prophetess whose wisdom was disregarded.

Mary had heard their stories a thousand times before, and she grieved for them.

Chapter 29

Collaboration

Morell had come to Handel's house prepared for a fight, though by no means anxious for one. He was of course grateful for the status attaching to this partnership and he badly needed the money, so he was always willing to make on the spot changes to fit the musical notation.

However, there were some points on which, he hoped, he would make a stand.

> 'We've wasted enough time!' cried Handel as the door closed behind Mrs Delany. 'No more visitors, Christoph, not the King of England himself! We must settle the ending, the fate of Agnes. The question is, how can a child's suffering atone for a father's action? How can we show this as an expression of God's love?'
>
> 'Agnes?' queried Morell, 'but surely her name is Iphis.'
>
> 'That's what I said,' growled Handel.

He marched into the composing room, grunted loudly, and returned with the brandy bottle whose contents he poured down his throat several times in succession.

'The mother clings to her child with all her strength, a she-wolf protecting her young. This quartet is the heart of it, *Spare Your daughter*, the child torn from her arms, the uncle and the lover pleading with the father who cannot, he simply cannot, unmake his vow! Oh God, the terrible suffering of that poor girl, I CANNOT BEAR IT! Yet it is for Jephtha we must reserve the most poignant aria, *Waft her, angels, to the skies*, for he is the agent of her death.'

'Her death?' ventured Morell, eyeing the rapidly emptying bottle with some alarm, 'but I thought you had accepted my point. We need not present it as a tragedy.'

'If not a tragedy, then what?'

'A moral lesson, that's what our audience nowadays expects of us. They are decent people of the middling sort; they know their Bible, but they do not always care to read it.'

'Yes, I know.'

'This makes it doubly important that we take the people with us, and you know as well as I do, what concerns them above all at this time are the dangerous divisions in our State.'

'Yes, yes, I know,' muttered Handel. He slumped down in a chair and swigged from the bottle.

'The threat to our peace not only from the Jacobite, but from the Deist heresy. You have said before that we must challenge it. And this is why, with respect,

Mr Handel, I urge that we show the Holy Spirit intervening directly in men's lives, the traditional teaching. An angel must save Iphis from death.'

'It's music I'm writing, not theology!'

'And not only that, you remember the heroine dying at the end of 'Theodora' didn't endear it to the audience.'

'That had nothing to do with it!'

'Can we risk another failure?'

'It was no failure! And with John Beard in the title role, they'll come to hear him, they always do.'

'Mr Handel, a death, even a courageous death, is not in fashion. To make the angel intervene is proper and decent. And then Jephtha's actions can be ascribed to Providence, through which God's loving ends are finally worked out; namely, victory and peace in Act 3. *The unity of Israel* – which our audience will of course see as meaning Great Britain – fully justifying the suffering and sacrifice.'

The red-robed cardinal leaned his head back on the chair and closed his eyes. He could not get out of his mind the impossible ideas he had stumbled upon in Holland: that there was no loving God ruling the world with justice, that the innocents of the world suffered for no good reason. He must, *he must,* find a way of dealing with this, if he was to compose this work!

His brow was deeply furrowed, and Morell wondered if he was praying. His lips seemed to be moving.

164

'God's loving ends,' he murmured. 'The Unity of Britain.'

'Yes, Mr Handel. Many of us believe the Almighty has chosen our nation to be His own people of Israel on this earth. We have a sacred duty to our traditions; our kings have an unbroken line of divinity going back to the days of King David.'

'And so you say that the whole truth is rooted in the past. Unmoving. Never growing. But *he* thought otherwise. He saw truth as an ever-growing seed.'

'*He*? Who do you mean?'

Oh, I beg your pardon, I need time to think.'

'Of course. You haven't slept all night, I believe.'

'Come back again tomorrow, will you, Morell?'

'Very well, then, if you're tired.'

'There's a good fellow.'

Chapter 30

The Great Mr Pope

When Handel opened his eyes again, he thought that the old manservant had come into the room bringing his morning cup of chocolate. Then he saw that it was Smith's more youthful figure bending over the fire, poking the dying coals into life. So it was evening, and his faithful Smith had not gone home.

He shivered. A rug had been placed over his knees, but his slippers had fallen off and his feet were very cold. He felt grateful to Smith, who seemed able to shrug off his little moments of impatience in a way that his father, Schmidt, unfortunately wasn't.

> 'Christoph, you're a good boy. If God had willed me to have a son, I hope he'd have been like you.'

Smith nodded, flushed with pleasure, but did not pause in his task.

> 'Remember when I gave you music lessons? You were afraid of me then. Oh yes, you were. Teaching, I confess, tried my patience. And we spoke in our native tongue, didn't we, because you hadn't learned English yet. How old were you when your father brought you to England?'

'I was eight, sir.'

Smith saw the coals sparking into a blaze, sat back on his heels and raised his eyes slowly to Handel.

> 'I never thought of it before, but you must have had a hard time. A German boy at school here with an unpopular German king. The English never quite accept us, do they, even if we change our name and nationality. Sometimes I feel they want *me* to quit their island, leaving my music here wrapped in the Union flag and marked *Property of the British Nation*!'

They both laughed. Smith got up and turned to face what looked like a dark mass in the quavering light of the fire. The room seemed emptier and bigger because the clutter of papers was hidden.

> 'Shall I play over what you wrote yesterday?'

> 'Of course not. I was tired, that's all. Now I've slept, I can read it for myself. And I shall not pinch those damnable glasses on my nose, whatever Mrs Delany says! I'll just rest here for a few minutes. Christoph, light a candle. I want you to read to me.'

> 'The Holy Book?'

> 'No, not tonight. I can recite the verses I need by heart. There's a book of poetry you'll find on my shelf, 'The Essay on Man' by Alexander Pope.'

Smith put a taper into the flames and carefully ignited the big fat candle in its brass holder on the table. He remembered sending out for large candles like these when Handel began to show signs of impaired vision. The moment would come when the truth would have to be faced, but Smith dreaded it.

He collected the book, sat down under the candle's glow, looked through the first marked page, then waited for further instructions. But the composer was not ready yet. He put down the bottle, leaned his head back on the chair and closed his eyes.

'I used to know Mr Pope quite well, did I tell you that?'

'Yes, I believe you have mentioned it.'

'We were both house-guests of my Lord Burlington – oh, it was 1715 or 1716. Little Mr Pope, with his crooked back, and eyes that were full of pain, but sparkling, always, with new ideas. It was a wonderful time, so many of us, musicians, poets, painters, architects, living in Burlington House, discussing, arguing, working. Mr Pope and his friends wrote my first English dramas, 'Acis and Galatea' and 'Haman and Mordecai' which were sung at the Palace of Canons at Edgware. Ach, how many English words have I set since then!'

'Very many, sir.'

'And do you know, Christoph, Mr Pope said he had no ear for music, and he claimed in his 'Dunciad' that English music was dull – except for mine, which he praised. So you see, he did have a good ear after all. Well, come on, read to me, we haven't got all night!'

'Sir, I find it puzzling. Mr Pope was a Catholic, you'd think he'd put the Holy Family at the centre of it, but right here in Epistle 2,' he says, *The proper study of mankind is man.*

'We live in puzzling times, my boy. Never before in history have people asked so many questions. And questions are dangerous, yes, *dangerous.* They can uproot the strongest tree. Valentius has tugged at my very root, damn the man!'

'Beg pardon, sir?'

'Look…you know that setting the Scriptures gives me more pleasure than all other composing, because even the fools who ask questions cannot doubt the evidence of their own ears! I think Mr Pope in this poem had the same desire as I do, to show the perfection of God. But he does it, rather, by exposing the weakness of man. Christoph, pass me the brandy, my mouth feels like sand.'

'Here it is but sir, with respect, your physician said—'

'*Doctors!* I've just about had my fill of them! Ah, that's better. Sickness of the body we dread, but it's a gift from God, a lesson in humility. It was his blindness that healed Samson's spirit; now there's a mystery if you like. And I suppose, with all his infirmities, Mr Pope knew better than most what it means to be frail. But he had the wit, you see, to draw great insights from his condition. I was thinking about this in regard to Jephtha.'

'Yes, sir?'

'How to make this foolish man the instrument of God's Will for his people, as I have done before with Saul, Samson, Solomon, they all had imperfections, but *this* man! To sacrifice his child, not out of obedience to God as Abraham made ready to slay Isaac, but because he made a rash vow to the Almighty. Should he not die for what he made her suffer at the hands of that loathsome beast? That pernicious FORNICATOR, forcing himself upon her, debasing his monkish calling, debasing religion itself!'

'Monkish calling? I don't understand.'

'You see, there must be a way of including everyone, even those who do not believe! If I could find a form of words, an expression of truth that all can accept, then the right music will come to me. Because it must be true for everyone, even those who reject the teaching…even Brother Valentius.'

'Brother who?'

'Supposing, just supposing he was right, that apostate monk. That there is no single truth, no solo voice, but a polyphony. No single right or wrong. Christoph, if we had soprani but no alti, tenori and bassi, there would be no Chorus.'

'No, sir.'

'Supposing we could find the right words. Beyond the wit of Thomas Morell, or myself.'

Handel, in the darkness outside the candle-glow, fell silent, though his thoughts were anything but silent in the stillness of the room.

> 'And then,' the voice rumbled from the darkness, 'I remembered Mr Pope and this great poem. Read it to me, read me the part about Man not seeing what is around him, and only hearing discord, because he is incapable of hearing the celestial harmony.'
>
> 'Where is this part?'
>
> 'Look there, look, boy, Epistle 1! The place is marked.'

> *All nature is but art unknown to thee,*
>
> *All chance, direction which thou canst not see,*
>
> *All discord, harmony not understood,*
>
> *All partial evil, universal good,*
>
> *And spite of pride, in erring reason's spite,*
>
> *The truth is clear: Whatever is, is right.*

Smith paused, and put the book down. Handel drew a long breath.

> 'I don't understand why our loving God should will the innocent to suffer. But Mr Pope reminds us that as mortals, we *can't* understand. We don't see the whole truth, because our minds are too small. Valentius said something like this, but his ideas were shocking…that we can't know what's good or bad, even questioning why God should be good. I know that God *means* good! But now I begin to think that

171

everyone does not…cannot…perceive truth in the same way.'

'Yes, sir.'

'Read me the Chorus Act 2 *How dark, O Lord, are Thy decrees*. I want to hear the exact words.'

Smith leapt to his feet, relieved that they were no longer discussing things he found impossible to grasp, and collected the 'Jephtha' text from the composing room. He wondered again why it was so important in these sacred works for Handel to believe completely in the words he was setting. Smith himself produced worthwhile compositions, but they were scarcely the mainspring of his life.

> *How dark, O Lord, are Thy decrees!*
>
> *All hid from mortal sight!*
>
> *All our joys to sorrows turning,*
>
> *And our triumphs into mourning,*
>
> *As the night succeeds the day.*
>
> *No certain bliss,*
>
> *No solid peace,*
>
> *We mortals know,*
>
> *On earth below.*
>
> *Yet on this maxim still obey:*
>
> *What God ordains, is right.*

Handel had been murmuring the lines as Smith read them as if hearing the music that would fit the words, and at the end he sat up and pointed triumphantly into the air.

> 'Ja, this is the resolution for Jephtha. Morell's last line, *What God ordains is right.* We are going to change it to Mr Pope's line, *Whatever is, is right.*'

> 'WHAT?' cried Smith, so astounded that he forgot to use a respectful tone. 'You – the composer of 'Messiah' – are going to remove the word *God* from an oratorio?'

> 'But what about those who *cannot* believe in God's promise through His Son? Are they to have no commerce with their inner spirit? I see now, it's not how we worship that matters, it's about feeling that *rightness* that is at the heart of things! You are breathing fast, Christoph. Are you shocked? Yes, you are. When I'm in the company of the great Mr Pope, I don't feel so alone. In contrast to the Reverend Thomas Morell, who sees everything in black or white!'

Smith was still reeling from Handel's extraordinary pronouncement! He did not understand it and knew that Morell wouldn't either.

But he believed Morell would accept the new wording, providing he was allowed to carry the day in the matter of the Angel. It was why their collaboration was fruitful. He knew, too, that despite his frequent jibes at Morell, Handel liked his librettist and that their partnership was warming into a kind of friendship. This was to be welcomed as the composer had few close friends, the rift with Schmidt being, sadly, unresolved.

'Oh, I thought you were pleased with Dr Morell this time. In fact, you said the contralto mother and soprano daughter would be ideal roles for Signora Galli and Signora Frasi.'

'Yes, yes, I may have said that. But for him everything is so simple, G minor or G major. This Angel of his who comes in at the end – I shall *insist* on a minor section in the middle of the aria, some connection with the tragedy of life. And now I shall rest here till we start work in the morning.'

'Wouldn't it be better if you went to bed? It's awfully late—'

'I don't need you to tell me the hour, insolent puppy! GET OUT OF HERE AND DON'T COME BACK!'

Smith yawned as he closed the door behind him. He didn't have his master's lust for life, or, for that matter, his obsessive zeal for truth. But he was thinking it was a good sign that the old man had started shouting at him again.

It proved he still had a reserve of strength to draw on for the disaster that was surely coming; and as Smith descended the broad wooden staircase, his yawn turned into a smile.

Chapter 31

A Cosy Supper

'But my dear,' said Mary, carefully avoiding what Patrick called her *wheedling-wife* tone. 'It can't do any harm and may do much good. William Bromfield is surgeon to St George's and the Lock Hospitals, and I'm told is very highly regarded. And it would only be to examine your eyes, you may not need treatment.'

'In which case, it would be a waste of his time and mine. You are gracious to suggest it, my dear, but I'm exceptionally busy at the moment. Really, I shouldn't have even come out tonight.'

Handel was beginning to lose patience. Dr Delany had gone off again to his duties in Ireland, so Mary had lured the lion out of his den with a promise of a cosy supper with some novel dishes, but they seemed to be taking a long time to prepare and he suspected the invitation was a ruse to get him to wash, shave and dress. He admitted that she had a point there: white heat composing left no time for details like washing. But after all, she was a loyal friend, and he knew he had been neglecting her of late.

'Well, there are other specialists. What about Chevalier Taylor? He attends the King both at St James's and in Hanover, surely his credentials are above question. Let me arrange a consultation for you. After all you are the *royal* composer and deserve *royal* treatment.'

What I deserve, he thought, is the main course, which would hopefully be more substantial than the green-pease pottage he had been already been served, scarcely enough for a sparrow. The main course must at the very least be a brace of partridge, or perhaps a leg of mutton and a calf's-head pie. And all this time Iphis was sitting on the desk in the composing room with her ink wet…the tonal relation was her G major, expressing innocence and serenity, to Jephtha's anguished E minor, and the C minor of his *Open thy marble jaws, O tomb.* He must find a way of drawing Jephtha's *Waft her, angels* into Iphis's key.

Mary had gained one objective; he had not absolutely refused to be examined by Chevalier Taylor, who practiced as an oculist all over Europe; but she could not yet drop the subject of Handel's health.

'Only a month till your Lenten season starts! And all this enormous extra work for 'Jephtha'. Wouldn't it be wise to postpone the premiere?' she asked, and seeing a steely look come into his eye, she added, 'or cut down the number of concerts?'

'Not possible. We've got 'The Choice of Hercules' ready and Beard's booked for, 'Alexander's Feast' *s*o I'll give them my new organ concerto. All my usual

176

subscribers have booked. More, I believe, than went to Mr Arne's organ concerto.'

'How thrilling!' she exclaimed, ignoring the reference to the Arne concert. 'Your concertos are always so popular.'

'Yes, I'm told some that some people come to the Oratorio just to hear me play the organ in the interval.'

'Oh, I'm sure that's not true!'

'I don't care why they come so long as they come.'

'I know you better than that, my dear. But I do long to hear you play again. When did you write the new concerto?'

'I shall write it when I can spare the time. And 'Esther' and 'Judas' are almost unchanged, they only need topping and tailing…talking of which – what on earth do you call *that?*'

Lizzie had come in bearing a large dish piled high with an elaborate concoction of green leaves topped with fried artichokes, pigeon wings, eggs, radishes, and roasted wheat-ears, which she placed ceremoniously in the centre of the table.

A second maid brought in a plate of sliced tongue with currant jelly, some potted beef tarts, a compote of apricots and a bowl of stewed carp. They both curtseyed and left the room.

'There,' said Mary smiling bravely. 'It's a mixed salad, quite a new concept in home dining. I've been reading a wonderful book, 'The Art of Cookery Made Plain and Easy' by Hannah Glasse.'

'The book's title does not lie,' remarked Handel drily.

'These simple dishes are known to be beneficial for the health. And they have the great benefit that women don't have to spend all their time labouring in the kitchen when they could be, and should be, improving their minds.'

Mary had not, in fact, taken the recipes from Mrs Glasse's book but had invented them herself in the hope that Handel would find he could enjoy nutritious food.

A good idea to improve women's minds. But not if it interferes with their cooking, thought Handel, as he sat down in his own room to a late-night snack of roast venison, veal fritters, plum pudding, and syllabub.

Chapter 32
How Dark, O Lord

The night of the thirteenth of February was windy. The window rattled in its casement, and on the desk the two fat candles which Smith had bought to shed greater light, flickered in their brass holders. The chimes of St George's sounded two o'clock, then three o'clock, a horse in the stable whinnied in its sleep, but Handel, bent over his desk, was aware only of the scratch of his quill on the paper and, now and then, the wine glass that raised itself to his lips. Act 2 was progressing too slowly! This was the heart of the work and must be the most perfect. He had, he thought, succeeded now in vesting Jephtha's long dramatic recitative *Deeper and deeper still,* with the full weight of tonal and emotional range, weaving this way and that as it followed each anguished thought from the despairing outcry of madness to heart-breaking tenderness.

But it was the final Chorus, the all-important one, *How Dark, O Lord, are Thy decrees* whose music must evoke man's submission to Divine Justice. The Chorus, it's very heartbeat bumping in a staccato rhythm, must distil the *Affekt* of fear, the weak mortal taking small and hesitant steps in the dark, and then gradually feeling its way through a sequence of ever-richer, ever stranger harmonies, into a beautiful resolution...*acceptance...peace*. Again and again he wrote notes and crossed them out, cursed the flickering candles. And then quite suddenly he found that the notes themselves were flickering, dancing like a swarm of insects, and flashing silver lights appeared in the corner of his left eye. Infuriating! He swatted them away with his left hand, but they were still there! Then a cloud covered his eye as opaque as black cloth, blotting out half of the room. He blinked furiously, tears falling onto his cheeks, wiped his eye angrily with his sleeve as if to wipe away the black mist, but there it stayed. The notes, the page, had flown away into the shadows, the very room had shrunk to a dreadful half-moon.

It was nearly five o'clock when Smith arrived with the manservant's hastily scrawled note in his hand, leaped from his coach and ran into the house, which was unnaturally bright with candles, taking the stairs two at a time. He could not get the servants to say how long Mr Handel was crying out before the physician was sent for. He could not speak with Mr Handel because his master was not aware of him. He had a heavily bandaged eye, like a soldier after a battle which has been lost, and was gulping almost continuously from a wine bottle.

When Handel had finally been put to bed, Smith tiptoed into the composing room and looked over the manuscript of 'Jephtha' lying open on the desk. The chorus *How dark, O Lord, are Thy Decrees* had been broken off in mid-cadence, and in the margin some German words were scratched in shaky but unmistakable handwriting: *Reach'd here on 13*

Febr 1751,unable to continue owing to a relaxation of the
sight of my left eye.

The habit of correcting what he had just written was so deeply ingrained that even at such a moment, Handel had crossed out the word *relaxation* and written s*o relax'd.*

Chapter 33

Scientific Treatment

Chevalier Taylor is travelling in his own comfortably sprung carriage to visit a patient. Naturally a physician of his stature should not go by public conveyance through London's streets on this squally winter's day, with wet leaves whipping up into the air, especially as his destination is the elegant environs of Mayfair. Is he not oculist to a host of dignitaries, including the King of Great Britain and Ireland? His Majesty, as everyone knows, has left England immediately after his son's funeral and returned to Hanover – to dally with his favourite mistress. King George the Second lacks dignity, in the Chevalier's estimation, he demeans his royal calling. But he is still, undeniably, a King.

Mr John Taylor, immediately on accepting the post of Royal Oculist and without waiting to be knighted, has been styling himself The *Chevalier* Taylor.

The vehicle he uses to travel about London is more discreet than the one in which he does his European tours. That one is painted over with huge images of eyes; and for the educated few who see him passing, the motto *Quit dat videre dat viver* (He who gives light gives life) is painted on the side of the coach. His approach to a town is heralded by placards and handbills advertising his willingness to wield the knife is return for the requisite cash. It is his normal practice to attract crowds by holding a rally in the town square, at which he performs the surgery, pockets the cash, and then quits town as fast as possible before the bandages are removed. This is a wise precaution because, as he once admitted to a friend, earlier in his career when he practiced as a surgeon in Switzerland, he had blinded hundreds of patients.

But who knows, really, if their blindness was due to his surgery?

Science is far too complex, too scientific, in fact, to be explained so simply. The patient may well have brought it on himself by removing his bandages too soon. Or because his sins had not been forgiven. Or because he had been cursed by a witch.

That fellow he operated on recently in Leipzig is a conundrum that continues to bemuse the Chevalier as he rolls through London's leafy squares. He was some sort of musician, just like the fellow he's going to visit now: a certain Herr J.S. Bach. He appeared to listen when the translator explained that the Chevalier intended to *couch* the eye – that is to say, in layman's terms, he would stick the flat end of a needle into the fellow's eyeball and push the cataract-clouded lens back into the posterior chamber, out of the field of vision. But it seems that Herr Bach just wasn't paying attention. At any rate he would not lie perfectly still, even after having strong spirits poured down his throat, and had to be held down on the table by four members of his numerous family. Naturally in these circumstances it hadn't worked, the procedure on both cataracts had to be carried out a second time. But the family claimed it hadn't worked then either, in fact they said Herr Bach was now in acute pain and had gone stone blind – though of course, they may have been saying this to get their money back.

None of the Chevalier's patients ever get their money back and neither, if it comes to it, will this fellow in Mayfair. To give money back would be an admission of guilt, quite ruinous for business.

The Mayfair musician is unfortunately also a foreigner with execrable English. On his last visit the Chevalier was subjected to an almost incomprehensible story about the patient's father who, he claimed, was a famous surgeon; though since he had never served a King, this claim was obviously spurious.

The patient himself is in the King's service and therefore merits the Chevalier's attention; if for no other reason, that as the King's Composer he can be charged a Royal fee.

But it is to be hoped the fellow has got himself properly dressed this time. It demeans the office of the Royal Oculist to examine someone who presents himself in bedgown and slippers!

*

'Incipient Gutta Serena, no doubt of it,' he announces, having peered into Handel's eyes for a few moments. 'Afflictions of the eye are either Gutta Opaque, clouded by morbid tissue, or as in your case Gutta

184

Serena, without too obvious swelling or discharge. The left eye has worsened since my last visit, I thought it would. The modern treatment is couching.'

'But Dr Taylor,' interposes that nuisance woman who always seems to insinuate herself into the parlour at these moments, despite his instructions to keep her out of the way, 'Is there not a less invasive procedure?'

'Less invasive? With respect, ma'am, what can a lady know of such things?'

'With respect, sir, I make it my business to know. And...' she hisses under her breath, 'though my friend must not hear this, the operation sounds barbaric, you would not do it to a dog!'

'Madam, it is practically painless. But of course, a lady cannot be expected to understand. It is for the *gentleman* to decide whether he wishes to avail himself of my skill.'

The Chevalier looks at the patient for affirmation but he, swaddled in that grimy red robe, with his hair ruffled, has turned to face the wall! He actually seems to have diminished in size, and to have resigned the whole question to this physically alluring but otherwise intolerable female. And even her expensive perfume cannot mask the unpleasant odours in the room, pipe smoke, coal smoke, and yes – a decided whiff of spirits! This corpulent fellow is undoubtedly a candidate for gout: the Chevalier wonders if he can bump up the fee by throwing in a gout tonic.

He puts down his quizzing glass, takes from his waistcoat a rose-coloured satin pouch, from which he extracts a large pinch of snuff; and feeling disinclined to ask for the lady's permission, since she shouldn't even be here, he snorts it loudly from a lacy wrist up each of his nostrils.

'I think, Doctor, that Mr Handel would prefer to discuss it with me before committing himself.'

'Sir, if I may address you directly! I have to warn you that without my treatment there is no doubt in my mind that in time, all sight will be extinguished. You will have to retire from public life.'

'RETIRE?' comes a rumbling at last from the scarlet cocoon. 'But I haven't finished my work!'

'Of course,' continues Taylor, stowing the snuff-pouch back in his pocket, 'it's not unheard of for musicians to perform without benefit of sight. The organist John Stanley has been blind from birth, and I am told that you never lose an opportunity of hearing him play. Without my services, the best you can hope for is to become Mr Stanley's partner at the organ.'

The cocoon suddenly unfurls and in one continuous movement the composer rises to his feet, larger than ever.

'Have you never read the Scriptures, sir? When the blind lead the blind, do they not both fall into the ditch?'

The woman smiles provokingly at this repartee. Clearly there is nothing to be gained while she is here.

'Sir, my time is very valuable. I am expected at the Palace within the hour. Pray, madam, ring for

186

someone to show me to my carriage, and you, sir, can instruct your assistant to write to me when you desire to have a *private* consultation. Your servant, Mr Handel. Good day, ma'am!'

Chapter 34

Breakdown

'MURDER! They said she murdered him, but it was *he* who murdered *her*!'

'Hush, hush, what is it, my dear, what are you saying?'

'She was innocent, an innocent child, and he took away her life!'

'George, you're ill, let me fetch a doctor—'

'Mary, listen to me! You have the True Faith; you know the power of prayer.'

'Yes, I think so, my dear.'

'All my life Jesu has been my sole guide, my comforter, till now...Oh!'

'What is it, George? Are you in pain?'

'O Mary, so much pain! If darkness is the Father's Will for me, then surely, I must submit to darkness. To defy His Will with remedies of science, that is not submission. But there's my vow, Mary, the vow I made long ago, to use my gift to praise Him, even to my last breath, and how can I write without sight? Oh,

Mary, *which* voice? Heaven heard my thoughts and wrote them down! IT MUST BE SO! Oh Mary, which voice?'

'You will know when the time comes. You always know—'

'It's a curse, Mary, he has cursed me with doubts, with his…his VALENTIAN HERESY that truth is not one, but many, that God speaks no more to mankind than to…to a blackbird! Mary, we have been friends so long – please, may I take your hand?'

'Come to my arms, George.'

'Oh, you are a good woman!'

'We shall pray together. Just as you used to do at home.'

'This madness cannot come from God, it's from the DEVIL!'

'Perhaps, my dear. We shall see.'

'I *tried* composing with one eye! I couldn't attach the tails, couldn't put the notes between the lines—'

'I know, I know. Your poor eyes are red. But weeping is good, so don't stop, let the tears flow. And one day, God will guide you again.'

'Mary, I…I can no more!'

*

'He's extraordinary,' says Mary to her husband, who has returned to London. 'A week ago I was greatly afraid, it seemed like a relapse into that state, you know, with the paralysis. Not his hand, this time, his mind. I was going to visit the poor man on his birthday and try to bring him some cheer. But that very day I got Smith's note saying Handel had written on the manuscript e*twas besser* which means, "somewhat better" – and on the strength of that, off he goes to the theatre and directs the entire performance of 'Belshazzar', if you please, *and* plays his new organ concerto! And now, barely a week later, I gather he has finished Act 2.'

'Thanks be to God!' says Patrick, 'He's found his direction and not least from you, sweetheart, with your caring ways. Will he be writing Act 3 now, do you think?'

'I intend he shall *not*,' declares Mary, 'before he has had a good long rest. He must go to Bath and take the waters, those treatments helped so much with his hand. And I shall see to it that he leaves the manuscript at home and that the servants don't let him wander off on his own!'

Lizzie was in the room, so Dr Delany pressed his knees into his wife's, under the table.

'It's good to be back,' he said. 'I know how troubled you've been. And it pains me, too, to see a towering man about to fall like a blinded Samson.'

'*Dark, dark, dark, amid the blaze of noon.* To think how he has overplied himself in music's cause! I'm not sure I could go and hear his 'Samson' now, it would be too dreadful.'

'Are you sure, dearest, he's strong enough for this excursion today?'

'Yes, an outing is just what he needs, and I have it all arranged. Lord Shaftesbury has lent his carriage and Smith will bring his master here as I instructed, wrapped in the winter cloak, hat, gloves and muffler and a rug over his knees, then you and I join them and ride together to where...yes, any time now the musicians will be assembling. Doubtless Mr Castrucchi will be rehearsing them extra thoroughly.'

'A surprise concert. How like you, Mary! Tis a cold day for the fiddlers' fingers but they'll be glad enough to play for him. And I suppose he'd best lose the habit of directing and learn to be an audience.'

This is an afternoon which, in later years, she often likes to remember.

It's past one o'clock when the carriage with its ornate Shaftesbury coat of arms, pulled by two glossy black cobs, leaves the sounds and smells of London behind and bounces along the rutted track across furrowed fields towards the little village of Marylebone. The day is raw but mercifully fine and clear, one of those days of slanting winter sun when the bare twigs seem to shiver with the promise of new life. Mary glances across the carriage to where Handel, sitting between her husband and Mr Smith, bounces stolidly like an upholstered statue. He had been too exhausted to protest when his servants trussed him up for the journey, and his face under the black three-cornered hat seems oddly expressionless. Mary hopes he is not still tormenting himself with this idea he called The Valentian Heresy. She has asked him to explain it, even to spell it out, but it still means nothing to her. All she knows is that he had clung to her like a lost child, and that she will move heaven and earth to lift his spirits.

She has briefed Signor Castrucchi on the programme she wants, some movements from the ever-popular 'Alexander's Feast', and the piece she knows as the Passacaglia, surely his most graceful and charming dance music. Mary had once seen the great Marie Salle dance it for him as an interlude in 'Terpsichore'; (a remarkable woman who had become a choreographer in her own right, a credit to her sex!) These joyful melodies will remind him of his past successes, they can't fail to warm his heart. And Castrucchi, who has led his orchestra for many years, can pause the players or quicken the tempo at the merest twitch of Handel's eyebrow.

Nobody speaks as they clatter down the Village Street, arriving at the high walls above which bare-branched fruit trees can be seen, and enter the Gardens by the north gate. At the centre is the great oval bowling green, encompassed by wide gravelled paths which are now empty, and little walks leading off to green enclaves with their box hedges and rose bowers which would be aromatic on a summer day and pleasantly peopled with strollers. It might seem a strange venue; but, as she explained to Patrick, she has chosen the almost deserted Marylebone Gardens in preference to Vauxhall, where poor Handel would be recognised and his unseeing eye tutted over, being convinced that fresh air and musical company will do him more good than a dozen physicians. Coming here off season also means there will be no cockfighting or dog-baiting or other horrible masculine pastimes that are known to go on behind the trees.

When they reach the Hall Signor Castrucchi comes out to meet them, bowing and beaming. Handel's face has now cracked into a picture of delighted wonder; he is heard to murmur *Vielen Dank* as he is almost carried down the steps by the Shaftesbury groom, and he shuffles indoors upheld on each side by Dr Delany and Mr Smith.

But once indoors, the inert Handel – as if a spell has been lifted – at once unfreezes into the man! He is cheerfully and loudly greeting these brother musicians with whom he has spent his most important hours, as if he has never, in the slightest, resembled a statue. Mary bustles into the kitchen to ensure the mulled wine is ready and that Miss Trusler, who has come in especially for her dear Mr Handel, is keeping her plum tarts and celebrated hot almond cheesecakes glowing on the range.

But it's when the refreshments have been cleared away and the little audience is seated at the front, that Mary has her reward; watching Handel, glowing and gratified as his work is played to perfection, she in turn glows. Despite Patrick's doubts, she has been right in every way. *Happy, happy, happy pair, none but the brave deserve the fair* rings out the full orchestra for Alexander; and then a concertante group of violins, flute, and cello gather in a family semicircle round the harpsichord to play the simple theme and variations that she knows as his 'Passacaglia'.

193

And yes, this really *is* Handel at his most delightfully gallant, the tune in triple time lightly accented on the second beat, a rhythm that would effortlessly lead the dancers to bow to each other, to genuflect, to touch hands as they passed, to glide across the floor, to circle each other with eyes interlocked...

She suddenly finds herself filled with longing! Her feet are pushing her to stand up, her knees are bending and straightening in time to the music, even as she sits!

How can anyone listen to this and *not* dance?

For a moment she actually contemplates pulling Patrick up and getting him to dance with her. But then she remembers that Patrick does not dance; it is perhaps the only absent pleasure in their marriage.

But later, Mary, she tells herself.

She would make sure that the later time came, one day.

Today belongs to Handel; and right now, she has to organise his safe passage home.

Chapter 35
Into the Mist

He arrived in Bath under the watchful eye of Smith one fine afternoon in March, and he was not too tired to admire the splendid sweep of the Nash terraces as the coach took him to his lodgings. Next morning, he insisted on walking on Smith's arm to the Communal Bath. Smith wondered how long it would be before Handel would take an interest in the news and gossip of the Spa, the daily breakfast clubs, card games and lectures, the nightly dances and concerts. Doubtless he would meet up with acquaintances in whose presence he was more likely to make himself swallow the nasty-tasting waters at the Pump Room; and after promenading down the shopping arcades inspecting the new fashions, they could on fine days sit outside the coffee houses listening to the town's excellent bands.

But for the present he was enjoying being a sleepy white whale, wallowing in the Great Pool in his muslin drawers and chemise, nibbling now and then on the healthful delicacies that the attendants floated around the pool on little trays. *It was perfect! Nothing to think about, and no-one. How long had he needed this?*

From there he was helped up the steps and he went back to the hottest of the Vapour Rooms to sit on a chair and dream. Just like an Italian summer! A man could sit here and let the years roll away down his body. As the chamber was full of steam, for once it didn't matter that he could barely make out the shapes of men as they emerged and disappeared in the mist.

What he didn't know, was that he was singing, continuously, and quite loudly.

> 'Excuse me, whoever you are!' boomed a voice from the mist, 'would you mind holding your tongue? I have come here expressly for some peace and quiet!'

> 'I beg your pardon, sir, I had no idea. You are right, this is no place for music.'

> 'Not that kind of music, anyway, it sounded foreign. We don't want any of that kind of thing in here!'

> 'No, of course not. Peace and quiet, I assure you, sir.'

> 'I'm obliged to you, sir, one scarcely meets with courtesy nowadays. And I suppose we all have our different tastes.'

> 'Quite so. Tell me, sir, what is your opinion of the musical taste in England?'

> 'Well, as to that, the best entertainment round here without doubt is this burlesque show 'The Dragon of Wantley'. You might still get a ticket – oh, it's so amusing! I believe it had a great run in London. The whole thing is a joke, making fun of Oratorio and all that serious stuff.'

'So…you are not of the opinion that Oratorio will become the new fashion?'

'You mean Saul and Samson and that kind of thing. Well, of course, the best thing about Oratorio is, you can have an evening's entertainment and come out feeling, you know, a better person, without actually having to sit through a church service. And the other thing is, it gives all those people who like singing in large groups, something to do with their time.'

'Yes. I never thought of that.'

'But personally, if I go out for the evening, I'd far rather go and see some fellow kicking the hell out of a dragon, wouldn't you?'

*

Mary was delighted with this story when Handel recounted it to her, especially when he said the little encounter had amused him for the rest of the day. But she saw that the treatment had resulted in no improvement in his eyes, whose very lids seemed to her to be beginning to harden, more and more resembling the stone eyes of his statue.

He played her over his new music for Act 3. She wondered what it must have cost him to set Jephtha's first recitative *Hide thou thy hated beams, O sun*, at such a painful time, when he was fast losing sight of the sunlit world.

The succeeding aria, *Waft her, angels*, she thought the most beautiful he had composed for many years: Jephtha's tender and anguished prayer for the daughter he is about to kill, the voice gently rising up to heaven in a heart-rending appeal.

For the final chorus, he explained to her, he had mustered all his strength to celebrate the great prize of national unity gained by the characters' sacrifice, culminating as expected in a Hallelujah Chorus.

Mary thought it a shame that so many who were now ecstatic over The Hallelujah Chorus in 'Messiah' had never heard his settings of it in other works. She especially loved *Your Voices Raise, Hallelujah*! In his Anthem 'O Praise the Lord with One Consent', the rollicking and bouncing motions of the Cherubim and Seraphim making her shoes rap on the floor – while the Israelites in 'Saul' singing Hallelujah she thought the most magnificent of all, lifting her almost physically up to the roof!

But in 'Jephtha' it was the girl, Iphis, with her lilting dance-rhythms expressing her physical, womanly joy in life, whose progress Mary had always watched with the closest attention, and she was not disappointed.

Her final aria *Farewell, ye limpid springs* was, as Morell had written it, a dismissal of the busy world on earth with its brief moment of joy, in favour of the brighter world of heaven to which she was bound.

But as she listened, Mary felt it was not the heroic renunciation that Handel's music lingered over; it was the pleasures of earthly life, the joy of cool springs and rivers, the green meadows and woods, to which he was singing a personal farewell.

Chapter 36
L'Allegro ed Il Penseroso

'It's good to be out in the countryside again. I have found London oppressive.'

'William and I are delighted you came,' said Jane Hogarth with her prettiest smile. 'It's been far too long, and you seemed quite buried in your work.'

'I was, ma'am. I have neglected my friends, and this Spring I have only seen Mr Hogarth at the Governors' meetings.'

'His subject is the great city, its reckless and terrible charms. But he stays in town only to make sketches for the scenes he paints here.'

'Little wonder, with your air so pure, and even the Thames beyond the garden smelling sweet. I would stay here all day listening to the birds.'

Handel and Mrs Hogarth were standing together under the portico of the house, as a fine summer rain was falling which put the stroll round the garden they had planned on hold. William was in the Painting Room over the coach – house at the bottom of the garden, where he would undoubtedly work until dinner, and Jane wanted to use this time on their own to talk to Mr Handel on a delicate subject; but she knew it must be approached gradually, and by a congenial route.

'Can you hear our lady woodlark? She often comes back to nest with us.'

'Yes, that was her, ma'am, that repeated ringing chime, the tight little trill. But now she flies off to a tree, and here comes the British virtuoso with his beautifully shaped mellow phrases, each one so different, the blackbird.'

The British virtuoso? Do you mean it was a blackbird you paired so wonderfully with the flute in Milton's 'L'Allegro'? Surely that was a nightingale.'

'Yes, but Milton was walking in the forest on a moonlit night when he enjoyed his nightingale. I don't think we're likely to hear one on a wet morning in Chiswick!'

'William and I loved your organ concerto with the two birds echoing each other. Everyone is clamouring to hear it.'

'Yes, I'm told they're calling it 'The Cuckoo and the Nightingale'. It helps sell a piece, you know, to have a name.'

'Do you often put birds into your music?'

'Whenever possible. In 'Rinaldo', my first London opera, the heroine sings an aria in a verdant woodland, and someone brought along a cageful of sparrows to fly among the trees as she sang.'

'What a novel idea!'

'Yes, but unfortunately, no-one had thought of how to catch the sparrows after the aria. The result was, they kept flying across the stage in all the later scenes where they were quite out of place and decorating the heads of the audience!'

'Weren't you furious?' cried Jane, laughing.

'Everyone always thinks I'm furious,' he said, smiling shyly. 'Perhaps because I shout. My cardinal fault, Mrs Hogarth, impatience.'

'Was that, perhaps, what went wrong, this time? I mean, with the boy?'

There, she had said it, sooner or later it had to be said, but oh dear – Handel's face had become a thundercloud! She had offended him! For it was she who had suggested the lonely old bachelor might adopt a foundling boy.

She and William had no children of their own, but they took great pleasure in fostering the foundlings, letting them romp through the garden, swing on the mulberry tree, play with their dog. Handel happened to be visiting at the moment when William was teaching an artistically gifted boy to draw…and the idea came to her that the composer might, perhaps, adopt a musical foundling to raise as his son.

But the experiment was short-lived. As Mary Delany recounted to Jane, after only a few days under Handel's roof the musically gifted boy ran away from the house never to return, leaving his benefactor baffled and embittered.

'And it didn't seem as if the failure was going to be explained now, Handel was snarling in guttural accents that sounded much more like High Dutch than English; '*Ze mother was vooled! The fazza was vooled! But I WAS NOT VOOLED! He was EIN SCHOUNDREL and EIN GOOD FOR NOTHING*!'

Oh dear, he really could sound terrifying! He must have terrified the boy, perhaps even raised his fist. How could this snarling, spitting man-mountain before her be the same compassionate man who was raising thousands of pounds to feed and clothe children?

It must be, she thought, because he lacked the experience of giving way to another. The years of fighting a lone path had robbed him of that skill.

But the next instant, to her great relief, there was another transformation: Handel smiled at her – and it was like the sun coming out from behind a cloud.

> 'I am impatient, ma'am, at this very moment. But please have no fear, I shall not shout.'

> 'Impatient?'

> 'To see Mr Hogarth's new work.'

> 'William is eager to show you. But we didn't know…if you could still…'

> 'I can still take pleasure in art, if he will kindly describe to me all the fascinating details that give his work such meaning.'

> 'He admires your work just as much, Mr Handel.'

'Though I've always known he dislikes the Italian taste. His 'Enraged Musician' makes fun of the music master who, some say, resembles my own Signor Castrucchi.'

'Let's say, we both greatly prefer your wonderful settings of Dryden and Milton. But you are a master of so many styles. Tell me truly, Mr Handel, is there any feeling you have expressed in Italian that cannot just as well be sung in English?'

'Well, jealousy, perhaps. And madness. Unfortunately, Mrs Hogarth, I've known all of these states. Otherwise, how could I make music for them?'

'But that's just why your Jolly Man lifts up our hearts, and why your Serious Man moves us to tears.'

'Though Milton, for good artistic reasons, conceived L'Allegro and Il Penseroso as two separate characters. It's far less comfortable, you know, when they are battling for mastery within one man. Perhaps,' he added, 'it is for this reason, above all, that we create.'

Chapter 37
The Cut

And so it has come, the hour of submission. My soul is in His keeping, but my body must surrender here.

The surgeon hovers over me, a vague shape, very long, very dark. I don't know which one it is, Bromfield, Taylor, Sharp, they've all prodded and poked my eyes, put stinging drops in to make them open and close and weep. But this one doesn't want conversation. He has something in his hand which he holds to my nose, and it makes me very sleepy.

Like Valentius did.

Brother Valentius.

But I don't think this is he.

It's too tall.

Too tall.

Is it my father?

My father, the surgeon, who stood above me like a great tree. He rocked me in his branches like I was a baby bird.

Or he could crush me with one blow.

He had about him…the Majesty of God.

But in the middle of the night when sick people came for help, I heard them shrieking, begging him, stop the pain! *and I thought him cruel* – he lanced them, made their blood spatter, he put leeches in their mouths, broke their bones –

To save them!

To save them.

And I heard my mother's tears, in her great love.

Chapter 38

Gifts

A woman is coming up the stairs and it's not one of my housemaids, I know their footsteps, quick and light about their duties, this step is firm and strong – *it's Mary!* She knocks at the door, comes in without waiting, and something lovely comes in with her…yes…a rush of flowers freshly picked from a garden, flowers wet with dew.

'Good morning, my dear, how are you?'

'Thank you, the pain is less today,' I tell her, breathing in the delicious scent. 'You've brought something sweet and fresh from the garden!'

Bless her, she holds the flowers up for me to sniff, and I stroke their silky petals which feel like the ears of dogs.

'I don't usually admit it,' she says, 'but there are times when real flowers are better than my paper ones.'

'Lilies! But summer has barely arrived…hasn't it? How can these be in bloom?'

'Under glass. Lord Shaftesbury had them picked from his glasshouse and his groom brought them up to town yesterday. I had Lizzie put them outside at dawn so I could bring the smell of morning into you.'

I can hear the skirts of her gown rustling about as she fills a vase from my jug of water and begins to arrange the blooms close to my chair. Her own perfume is rich, exotic, it hovers warmly around the cold flower smell.

'How kind you are, and how kind of his Lordship. I would like to thank him.'

'I will write to him with your thanks.'

'I could show my gratitude better by playing for him!'

I fidget with my dressing which is heavy and hot, and I feel Mary's cool hand close over mine.

'No, my dear, better not. Even if it's uncomfortable.

You remember my accident in Holland? A hermit looked after me, and whatever the treatment was, the bandage on my head got smaller and smaller. But here in London it gets bigger and bigger.'

'Though I'm bound to say, *you* are getting smaller and smaller.' She pats my stomach. 'Yes, your figure quite diminishes.'

'When I was composing,' I explain, 'it took a lot of fuel to stoke up the fires. But with no work to do, I don't seem to need this mortal flesh.'

'No work to do? My dear friend, never say that! Why don't you take the waters again? They are sure to refresh your muse.'

'No! No more! I have taken the waters at Tunbridge Wells and Bath and Cheltenham and Scarborough. I have put on a muslin shift and swum in lakes of steam. I have forsworn meat and nibbled fruits and swallowed sulphurous draughts from hell. I have submitted to three surgeons, each time with greater fear and pain and I have endured all this because while there is music for me to write, I must write. But today this bandage will be removed…and it will be the last. I shall do as a true Christian should, and submit to His will.'

'But are you sure,' she says, her rustling skirts seating themselves on the chair next to mine, 'that it is His will? Look at all you've done, even without sight, performed 'Messiah' every Lent for the Foundlings, given 'Jephtha' to the nation just as you planned with Galli and Frasi and John Beard.'

'I don't think it was understood.'

'The music was loved! It is very fine, very different from the others but no less wonderful for that. And didn't you tell me you banked £600 after the first performance? You won't persuade me it was a failure.'

'Listen. Someone's coming up the stairs.'

Smith is coming to see me this morning, with a long-postponed visitor – who I am very anxious about. But these footsteps aren't Smith's.

'I think it's Dr Morell.'

He pauses at my door and knocks softly. I can hear my servant telling him that it's all right to go in because the surgeon isn't here yet. But there is another pause, and he knocks again. We both call for him to enter, the door opens and Morell walks in, with…I can hardly believe it, *he, too*, has thought of bringing into my sick room a cheering smell (how kind they all are!) which I recognise at once. He puts the little orange with its strange scaly skin into my hand, greets Mrs Delany formally, then asks me to accept this small gift with his compliments. Mary says, yes, it is certainly small. But I hold it to my nose and sniff it *rapturously*. Orange citrus! The little grove at Vignanello when I was a composer for the Marchese Ruspoli. I can feel the sun now, beating warm on my bare head in the early morning. I used to sit under the orange trees with this beautiful scent in the clear blue air, and watch the fountains, and then they'd bring my breakfast. Ahhhh!

> 'Though it isn't really my own gift,' says Morell, accepting one of the chairs. 'I am the bearer of it from a vendor at Covent Garden, where I go sometimes to see if they have any unwanted edibles to give away, and when I mentioned I was coming here, the woman positively insisted that you, *the noble Mr Handel* as she called you, should have this, and it's quite undamaged. She said they all miss seeing you walking to the opera house, and that your tunes more than anyone's have set their feet a-tapping these many years past. Oh yes, and she said this fruit can, with a little ground sugar, be crushed into a cordial that is agreeable and wholesome for invalids.'

Mary cries out that I am not an invalid, I am in recovery! But either way, this is a beautiful gift, more than my friends can imagine.

Mary gets to her feet, and I can hear her start to re-arrange her lilies in the vase; though she really doesn't need to demonstrate how indispensable she is to me. Seeing that both Mary and I have gone quiet, Morell fills the silence.

> 'It's such a fine morning, I walked here past the Foundling Hospital. They say tickets for 'Messiah' sold even faster this year, and the fund has grown to ten thousand pounds. Think of it, *ten thousand pounds* to feed and clothe the children, and educate them, and teach them trades! Not only do your oratorios carry the True Religion to every English-speaking land, but your acts of charity have created a new fashion: giving to the poor.'

> 'It's true, my dear,' agrees Mary, 'the Beau Monde positively push their way into the Chapel like so many bejewelled piglets.'

> 'Let's hope,' I say, 'that both charity, and my music, will survive.'

> 'Your music will live forever!' cries Mary.

> 'Will it? I've still got ears, I hear the new music, the *Galant* style with its clean simple line, the abhorrence of counterpoint. It seems people nowadays don't want to listen – they just want to dance! Even the keyboard is changing. Some while ago at Mr Donellan's house I played a new instrument that has just been invented: *the fortepiano.*'

'The *loud-soft*?' says Mary. 'What is it like?'

'Strange,' I reply, 'such a heavy action. I don't think people will have the strength in their fingers to play it. A curiosity, merely. Ah, here is Christoph coming upstairs – and he has someone with him. Can I please ask you both to withdraw for a little while? What this gentleman and I have to say to each other, must be said in private.'

Chapter 39

A Charitable Act

Smith, having shown his father into the parlour, is about to leave the room when surprisingly, Handel motions him to stay; so he goes to the window and looks out over Brook Street.

Though it will be impossible for him not to be involved in the reconciliation, *if* that is what happens. An exchange of greetings in formal German has taken place, but now the conversation is faltering. Perhaps Handel wants him here in case it breaks down altogether. At any rate the two friends need to be reconciled: His father is deeply unhappy, and Handel must deal with his own bitterness, he must wipe his slate clean for the journey to heaven.

It's he, Smith, who has brought these two together, the two most important men in his life. It was when Handel told him he was changing his Will to leave a large bequest to him, instead of his father, Smith knew he had to act. After all, what would people say? That the son had wormed his way into Handel's fortune at the expense of his own father?

He can hear his father's slow, insistent voice rising now...*for years, Handel has treated him little better than a SLAVE! Heaping more and more copying, more arranging, more distributing of parts onto him for the same PALTRY wage, exploiting his loyalty, and his son's loyalty.* Handel's voice rises higher and louder, edged by tears of self-pity…*HOW could Schmidt have done it? To have taken a blind man for a walk in Tunbridge Wells and then, just because of some harsh words, to have abandoned him there in the middle of the busy street? ABANDONED HIM TO ALMOST CERTAIN DEATH?*

Smith is patient, he knows that steam has to be let off, so he gives himself up to imagining the pair as they must have been as university friends. What would they have been like?

He sees his father, now so grey and bent, striding along a street in Halle, a tall figure with a full head of long, curling dark hair, his eyes alight and laughing; and matching him step for step, the slim, strikingly handsome youth Handel, a tall grey wig falling over his blue cloak and an almost feminine sweetness about his smile, just as he was painted in the Platzer portrait. How many Steins must they have sunk together! How many boat races on the river Saale, how many hours stolen from lectures to sneak into the local churches and take it in turn to try out the organs. The pipes they must have smoked, the sighing over musty law books, the testing each other on abstruse points by candlelight.

But quite suddenly the youths slide back into the past.

Two old men are sobbing in each other's arms.

*

214

While Smith is showing his father out of the house, Mary and Morell are re-admitted to the parlour. They have been waiting outside the room, not far away; and while Morell has closed his ears to the shouting, Mary has tried to make out what she could of the German, which is *not* one of her languages, in case Handel needs to talk to her about it later.

But as Smith immediately comes back upstairs and joins them, she decides not to refer to it.

'What time do we expect the surgeon?' she asks, for their general benefit.

'Very soon, ma'am,' says Smith.

'It's only right that he comes in person to remove the dressing,' she declares, 'it must be done expertly so as not to chafe the wound. Besides, he owes Mr Handel a favour, doesn't he, Mr Smith.'

'Yes,' agrees Smith, 'we are giving 'Judas Maccabeus' on behalf of the Lock Hospital, a charity of which this surgeon is the founder. I shall endeavour to direct the musicians as Mr Handel would wish.'

'*The Lock Hospital!*'

Handel and Mary are shocked by this exclamation from Morell.

'Surely Mr Smith is not suggesting that one of our oratorios, based on Holy Scripture, should be used to support that den of vice? Where no decent clergyman will ever set foot? Where women of the streets go to die without even having made confession! To die of…of sinful disease…'

215

'Of the pox,' put in Handel. 'These poor creatures have the pox, Dr Morell.'

'Really, sir! To use that word in the presence of a lady—'

'Oh fiddlesticks!' cries Mary, already on her feet. 'It's a wonderful place! It treats both male *and* female sufferers of venereal disease. How do you suppose, Dr Morell, these women catch it in the first place?'

'It's not something I have ever wished to think about—'

'One man of unbridled passion can infect dozens of innocent girls, ruining their lives! I say those *decent* clergymen of yours should stand up in the pulpit and denounce these men! They should tell the wives what their husbands get up to, they should make the fathers pay for their pox-infested *bastards*!'

It is probably fortunate that at that moment there is a knocking at the door and the arrival of the surgeon is announced.

Mrs Delany, fanning herself furiously, goes to the window and sits down on a chair; Dr Morell, feeling confused, goes and sits beside her, but they avoid each other's eyes. Smith stays standing behind his master.

Chapter 40

Beginning the Future

Praise God in His infinite mercy!

THE VALENTIAN CURSE IS LIFTED!

Prayer, the care of my friends, and those happy visits to the countryside have renewed that sweet breath of God that blows through us when we are our best.

And now, having got the better of Schmidt, I am more than ready to take on this surgeon. Whatever he may do to my flesh, I will have an answer in the spirit. Of course, with my eyes bandaged I don't see the man enter my room, but my hearing, which was ever as keen as a wild animal's, can now in my sightlessness paint me pictures that transcend this mortal world.

And so I hear the tall, dark physician in his long cloak moving swiftly over to me. His piercing eyes look down straight through the bandage into my eyes; he appears satisfied, and he opens a black velvet bag, takes out more rolls of bandages and stacks them on the table.

Then, from behind a green velvet curtain which I must say that I've never noticed before, a host of miniature attendants fly up like a flock of sparrows, two of them carrying a tub of paste between them in their claws and others carrying brushes in their beaks which they leave on the table before disappearing again behind the curtain.

And…ah! My nose twitches as sweet puffs of pink rose-scented smoke come shooting up from behind the curtain; and I perceive now that a gigantic golden palace has been painted on it, and in each corner of the palace a fat cherub with golden wings blows his golden trumpet against a sky of brightest blue. Marvellous! These are colours I have not seen for years!

Yes, it's the King's Theatre in the Haymarket, scene of my greatest triumphs, it must be a set for one of my forty operas – *but which one?* I smell the buzz of an expectant audience, the musk rose of a hundred candles shimmering and waving around the stage. Which of my gorgeous singers will stride out? How loud will the applause be?

And now the biggest of the cherubs puffs out his pink cheeks and blows a delightful fanfare, causing the others to gurgle happily and kick their fat little legs.

'Ah ha!' exclaims the surgeon in a tone I almost recognise, 'Here we are at the Transformation. Now we shall find you, Mr Handel, for better or worse. Mrs Delany, you can't stay here. Kindly leave the room.'

'How dare you dismiss me!' I hear Mary cry, 'I may be able to help!'

'Madam, ladies have no place in a surgical theatre, your idle chatter would be distracting. And Morell, you'd better leave too, we don't want any writer fellers fainting during the operation. But you, Smith, you can stay. I may need you to help me hold him down.'

'Hold him down?' shouts Smith from far away. 'What operation? Haven't you come here to remove the bandage?'

'Oh no, sir,' replies the surgeon calmly. 'The operation to be performed is of quite a different nature. Don't you understand? Mr Handel is no ordinary patient, he's a historical personage. He's going to die soon in any case.'

He begins to wind thick white bandages round my face, which is strange and frightening. I can hear Smith's voice shouting, trying to stop what is going on.

'Christoph!' I try to shout, beginning to struggle, beginning to panic. 'Don't let them do it, I CAN'T BREATHE!'

'Stop!' screams Christoph, and I can feel his hands clawing at the bandages, trying to tear them off, 'By what right do you muffle him up like this?'

'Stand back, Mr Smith!' commands the surgeon. 'You can't stop this process; it happens to all Britain's great men. Come on, boys, do your work.'

Two of the attendants re-appear with brushes and paste which they begin to slap all over my body. The surgeon stands by, giving directions.

'That's it: left leg pointing forward, right elbow leaning on the score. Mind the folds of the cloak. A bit more on this side. Good. He's getting quite rigid now. Be careful with the face! We want his eyes looking as though he can still see. The paste dries in seconds, leaving a nice marble finish.'

'A death mask!' cries Smith. 'But he isn't dead yet, *you're killing him*!'

The surgeon, rather offended, says, 'I am conferring immortality on him.'

'But how will anyone ever find him in there? Mr Handel! It's Christoph, CAN YOU HEAR ME?'

My dear boy kneels beside me and weeps brokenly.

And now the surgeon taps my head.

'See? Nice and hard. He's ready to go on his plinth in Westminster Abbey. And can't you see how much better this is? The whole nation can gather at his feet and sing his praises. Maybe twice a year, Christmas and Easter; it wouldn't be the same without him.'

An orchestra strikes up 'Messiah' and a choir bursts into *The Hallelujah Chorus;* at which the surgeon opens the black velvet case, takes out his copy of 'Messiah' and joins in the bass line with gusto.

*

But it's strange how quickly I grew accustomed to my place within a greater entity. Even when my bones had been interred and my monument erected with due solemnity in the Abbey, I remained in my house; and it was here that I learned that both 'Theodora' and 'Jephtha' became much-loved works in my repertoire, and that all my oratorios were eventually given fully staged performances. It was here that my subsequent history unfolded, which I found quite as fascinating as anything in my former life.

In no time the little parlour began to fill up. First to arrive were the music societies of Oxford, Cambridge, Lincoln, Canterbury, Exeter and Salisbury, followed by the Three Choirs Choral Festival singers, all trying to push their way past each other towards the sparse items of seating. Several of the more enterprising singers managed to squeeze inside the bookcase, while a soprano and a tenor lay end to end on top of the harpsichord!

The arrival of a further 513 performers for my 1784 Commemoration caused a certain degree of consternation; but this was partially resolved by members of the wind section hanging from the picture rails. The Altos, now almost entirely female, went down to the kitchen for a sectional rehearsal and were soon being requested to make cups of tea; while the timpanist took his equipment up to my bedroom where he could practice in peace.

In successive years, Festivals of my Music would swell in grandeur until the pinnacle was reached in 1883, when an orchestra of 500 and as many as 4000 singers tried to force their way down Brook Street. It was soon realised that a large fleet of horse-drawn omnibuses must be hired to take them from my house to The Crystal Palace, where a massive volarium or false roof had been erected with special resonators to amplify the sound. This was just as well because the audience, over the five days of the festival, totalled 87,769.

The management justified these enormous numbers partly on monetary grounds, as some of their receipts still went to charity, but partly too, because, as one of my biographers said, my Oratorio had become Britain's public assertion of the fundamental truths of religion – almost a substitute for religion. Richard Wagner wrote that it was by attending a Handel Oratorio that he came to *understand the true spirit of English musical culture, which is bound up with the spirit of English Protestantism... everyone in the audience holds a Handel piano score in the same way as one holds a prayer-book in church.*

Conversely, Edward Fitzgerald (a neo-pagan living in Victorian England) who attended one of these heavyweight performances, was so disgusted that he pronounced my sacred music to be both tedious and insincere! And he managed to persuade successive generations that I was *a good old pagan at heart!*

But, at the farthest edge of the universe, a small number of my admirers began to turn their footsteps back to the little parlour.

And I am glad to know that they heard in my work not only a joyous outpouring of creative power, but also a personal interpretation of mankind's spiritual life, wrought by a man who had opened the door of his heart to people of all faiths, and none.

*

The last time I saw Mary Delany was in a little clearing in a wood. She had asked me, in a dream, to meet her there. It was a summer's day and the trees were in full leaf, which bestowed a gentle green shade on the small group of musicians grouped in a semicircle round the harpsichord, a flute, two violins and a cello.

As a concession I had let Mary hand-pick the musicians, and a curiously seductive group they were, dressed like nymphs in long black gowns cut away at the back and fitting tightly over their young hips and breasts. If these were the musicians of the future, I was all in favour – providing these women could play my Passacaglia *perfectly* – and they did.

A theme with variations in triple time lightly accented on the second beat, a rhythm that led us, she and I, to bow to each other, to genuflect, touch hands as we passed, glide across the floor, to circle each other with eyes interlocked.

I enjoyed making her happy.

The supreme pleasure of giving pleasure!

Epilogue

Your Lord is waiting for you, good Christian that you are, just as you waited for Him on your bed in Brook Street until Good Friday before drawing your last breath, so that you might meet Him as He ascended.

You have seen, haven't you, that the passing of the body is nothing, the merest inhaling and exhaling of the earth. But on your way forward you want to know (of course you do) if she is well, that innocent child you met with several times in your life, whom brutal forces continue to crush, again and again.

I can only say that here, all things are well. It's the only way to speak of something which is beyond the power of earthlings to apprehend.

You call this place, The Beauty of God.

And I tell you that the beauty *you* create is a gift to eternity, whether you are a human being, a daffodil, a mountain, or a star.

Select Bibliography

Memoirs of the life of the late George Frederick Handel, John Mainwaring, Dodsley, 1760, repub. Travis and Emery 2007.

Anecdotes of George Frederick Handel and John Christopher Smith, William Coxe, London, W. Bulmer, 1799

The Letters of Handel, ed. E.M. Muller, Cassell, 1935

Addison and Steele, Selections from The Tatler and the Spectator, ed. R.J. Allen, Rinehart, 2nd ed. 1970

The Provok'd Wife: The Life and Times of Susannah Cibber, Mary Nash, Hutchinson, 1977.

Coram Children: The London Foundling Hospital in the Eighteenth Century, New Haven, Yale University Press, 1981.

Handel and his World, H.C. Robbins Landon, Weidenfeld and Nicolson, 1984.

Handel, Christopher Hogwood, Thames, and Hudson, 1984

Handel, the Man and his Music, Jonathan Keates, Victor Gollancz, 1992.

The Cambridge Companion to Handel, ed Donald Burrows and Rosemary Burrows, C.U.P. 1997

Handel as Orpheus, Ellen Harris, Harvard, 2001.

Music and Theatre in Handel's World, Burrows D and Dunhill R, OUP, 2002.

Evening in the Palace of Reason, James Gaines, Harper, 2005.

Mrs Delany: her life and her flowers, Ruth Hayden, British Museum Press, 2006.

'*Was George Frederick Handel Gay*?' Gary C. Thomas in Queering the Pitch, 2nd ed. Routledge, 2006

George Frideric Handel, Marian van Til, Wordpower, N.Y. 2007

Behind Closed Doors: At home in Georgian England, Amanda Vickery, Yale U.P. 2009

Cover images

Photograph of a miniature portrait of the composer Georg Friedrich Handel (1685-1759) by Christoph Platzer. Painted circa 1710 when Handel was about 25.
https://commons.wikimedia.org/wiki/File:Georg_Friedrich_H%C3%A4ndel_as_a_young_man.jpg

Portrait of Handel by Thomas Hudson, 1747
https://commons.wikimedia.org/wiki/Category:Portrait_paintings_of_Georg_Friedrich_H%C3%A4ndel_by_Thomas_Hudson#/media/File:Georg_Friedrich_H%C3%A4ndel.jpg

Philip Mercier's portrait of Handel
https://commons.wikimedia.org/wiki/File:Handel-Mercier.jpg

Louis-François Roubiliac's statue of Handel, formerly in Vauxhall Gardens, now in the Victoria and Albert museum
Photo taken by Helen Dymond

Notes and References

1. Ch.1. Handel was said to be able to swear fluently in five languages.

2. Ch.4. This painting in the Hermitage Museum, St Petersburg, is attributed to da Vinci, today it is called the Madonna Litta after the Milanese family of Litta who owned it in the nineteenth century.

3. Ch.7. Baron Wassaneur-Oppdam's Pleasure Garden: details from the James Harris Travel Diary 26 July 1732 in 'Music and Theatre in Handel's World,' Burrows D. and Dunhill R, OUP, 2002:03.

4. Ch.7. The key of Eb major with its three flats represented The Trinity for Bach, Handel, and Mozart.

5. Ch.8. Mary likens herself to Iphenigia in her Autobiography 1:20 in Molly Peacock 'The Paper Garden' Bloomsbury USA, 2010:80.

6. Ch.9. Letters of Charles Jennens to Edward Holdsworth, 1743, in Hogwood.C. 'Handel,' Thames, 1984: 182–183: 'His Messiah has disappointed me, being set in great hast, tho' he said he would be a year about it and make it the best of all his Compositions. I shall put no more Sacred Words into his hands, to

be thus abus'd... 'tis still in his power by retouching the weak parts to make it fit for publick performance, and I have said a great deal to him on the subject, but he is so lazy and so obstinate, that I much doubt the Effect.'

7. Ch.9. The outrage of some churchmen that attended the London premiere of Messiah in 1743 explains why for some years Handel used the alternative title A new Sacred Oratorio: 'An Oratorio either is an Act of Religion, or it is not; if it is I ask if the Playhouse is a fit Temple to perform it in or a Company of Players fit Ministers of God's Word... if it is not perform'd as an Act of Religion but for Diversion and Amusement only... what a Prophenation of God's Name and Word is this, to make so light Use of them!' Letter to The Universal Spectator, in Hogwood, 180–181.

8. Ch.9. Handel's Letter to the Daily Advertiser of 17 January 1745, cutting his season short, amounts to a fulsome apology and pays generous tribute to his adopted country:

    Sir, having for a Series of Years received the greatest Obligations from the Nobility and Gentry of this Nation, I have always retained a deep Impression of their Goodness. As I perceived, that joining good Sense and significant Words to Musick, was the best Method of recommending this to an English Audience; I have directed my Studies that way, and endeavour'd to shew, that the English Language, which is so expressive of the sublimest Sentiments is the best adapted to any of the full and solemn Kind of Musick. I have the Mortification now to find, that my Labours to please are become ineffectual, when my Expences are considerably greater. To what cause I must impute the loss of the publick Favour I am ignorant, but the Loss itself I shall always lament. In the meantime, I am assur'd that a Nation, whose Characteristick is Good Nature, would be affected with the Ruin of any Man, which was owing to his Endeavours to entertain them. I am likewise persuaded, that I shall have the Forgiveness of those noble Persons, who have honour'd me with their Patronage, and their Subscription this Winter, if I beg their Permission to stop short, before my Losses are too great to support, if I proceed no farther in my Undertaking; and if I entreat them to withdraw three fourths of their Subscription, one Fourth Part only of my Proposal having been perform'd.'

9. Ch.11. 'The great Luther…musical scale.' From J. Gaines, 'Evening in the Palace of Reason,' Harper Perennial, 2005: 43–49.

10. Ch.12. Handel's relationship with Mattheson is attested in Hogwood. C. 'Handel,' Thames, and Hudson 2004:22–26, and Keats J. 'Handel, the Man and his Music, 'Gollancz, 1992: 34–40.

11. Ch.13. Handel's affair with La Bambagia in Hogwood, Ibid, 37–39 and Keates, Ibid, 34–40.

12. Entr'acte, Covent Garden Piazza as 'The Great Square of Venus' painted by Samuel Scott, colour

plate in Cruickshank. D. 'The Secret History of Georgian London,' Windmill Books, 2009, Ch. 10.

13. Entre'Acte, Susannah performing as Juliet and the Wars of the Theatres in Nash.M. 'The Provok'd Wife,' Nash.D. Hutchinson, 1977: 254–257.

14. Ch.25. Handel is dubbed 'The Old Buck' in the correspondence of the Harris and Shaftesbury families. The 3rd Earl's book Characteristicks of Men, Manners, Opinions, Times was published in 1711.

15. Ch.39. Schmidt's complaining that Handel treated him as a slave in Burrows. D. and Dunhill. R, ibid: 171. Letter of Schmidt to James Harris 11 October 1743: 'My manner of writing of Mr Handels great merit in musick shall always be the same, though I cannot say so much of his behaviour towards me, and according to his repeated promises I expected a better reward for 24 years of slavery and services I have done him.'

16. Ch.40. For Handel's vision of his musical legacy I am greatly indebted to the research details in Hogwood. C. Ibid, pps. 232–256. The Wagner quotation is cited by Hogwood as coming from Wagner's 'My Life,' English edition, 1911:634–5.

GEORGE FREDERICK HANDEL Esq.ʳ
born February XXIII. MDCLXXXIV.
died April XIV. MDCCLIX. *L.F.Roubiliac inv.t et sc.t*

Handel's monument in Westminster Abbey shows him holding the
score of the aria *'I know that my Redeemer liveth'* from his most
famous work, *Messiah*. His birthdate is given as 1684 following
the pre-1700 Calendar.